A Shower of Summer Days

Books by May Sarton

A Shower of Summer Days

May Sarton

W · W · NORTON & COMPANY · INC ·

NEW YORK

Copyright © 1952 by May Sarton. All rights reserved. Published simultaneously in
Canada by George J. McLeod Limited, Toronto.

Printed in the United States of America.

First published as a Norton paperback 1979.

Library of Congress Cataloging in Publication Data
Sarton, May, 1912–
A shower of summer days.

I. Title.
PZ3.S249Shc   1979   [PS3537.A832]   813'.5'2
ISBN 0–393–00925–4 pbk.   79-1140

1 2 3 4 5 6 7 8 9 0

A Shower of Summer Days

AT LONG last in early June the Gordons were expected home at Dene's Court, the house in Ireland which Violet Dene Gordon had inherited. In twenty years she and her husband had come back twice from Burma on short leaves, but there had been no time to settle in, or to take the estate in hand. They seemed to the village people as restless as migratory birds, welcome enough visitors, but still only visitors. Would Miss Violet ever come home to stay, they wondered walking through the demesne on Sundays, pausing to look up at the blank windows shuttered from inside, at the tennis court overgrown with weeds, or to talk with the always despairing Cammaert, the one man left in charge of the gardens. He did not think of himself as a hero (that boy with his hand in the hole in the dyke), but as a matter of fact it had been a long lonely struggle to keep even a semblance of order against the rising tide of weeds. It had made him angrily taciturn, permanently at bay, so instead of giving the children flowers he shouted at them,

"Go ahead, take the roses, damn you. Who cares?" And stamped off, not looking back, not looking to see what they took, so more often than not they were too overcome with the possibilities to pick at all. The rose petals fell in the rain; the sweet peas withered on their stalks.

But finally the news percolated through that Burma was withdrawing from the British orbit, from Charles Gordon's orbit, this meant to the village consciousness. The postmaster saw in an old issue of the *Times* an editorial about the nationalizing of teak, and about the pity it was that all the British engineers and experts were being shown the door. There would be no one to train new men.

"Teak, that's Mr. Gordon's business surely," the postmaster announced in the pub. "So we can expect them home any day now," he said, like an oracle, hardly believing his own words, so that he was more astonished than anyone when rumors and conjectures gave way to letters from the Gordons and finally cables. "Didn't I tell you so?" the postmaster said, awed by his own prescience. "It's a strange thing how I felt it in my bones," he said, forgetting all about the evidence in the paper.

Annie Ryan, pensioned off and living in the village, made her way over to Mrs. O'Connell's in triumph with the letter announcing the Gordons' definite intentions, and Mrs. O'Connell opened a bottle of port to celebrate the news. Finally three months later, out of the blue, came a phone call through the post office so the whole village knew that Annie had been asked back, at least till the Gordons were settled in.

"All I could say was 'Yes, Miss Violet,' as if they'd never been away . . ." Annie told the group who had converged on the post office as the news spread that

4

Annie was talking to London. "And how I'll ever manage, what with the rheumatism, the dear Lord only knows." She was overcome now with the enormity of what she had undertaken, the huge house, empty all these years, damp everywhere. Yet the house was a friend; she had been cook there for almost half a century, all told. More even than Miss Violet, the house and her feeling for the house had made her answer as she did without hesitating. She couldn't bear even to imagine a stranger in her kitchen, someone who would not know how things had always been done, someone who would not see the glory of it for the mildew, someone who could not people it with the children now grown-up, with the parents and grandparents, now dead. "No one at all would do but myself," Annie said, rubbing ointment into her stiff knee as if preparing for a race.

Now lists of things to be done flew over from the English houses where Charles and Violet were staying: remind Cammaert to have lettuces started in good time; air the linen and blankets; clean the silver; get in coal; keep fires burning in all the rooms, the lists said in Violet's decisive hand—as if Annie needed to be told these things.

Every day Annie went over from the village and into the icy house, forgetting her rheumatism by the time she was halfway in a fury of satisfaction, and reminding Maire constantly of what they would have to do next. She had imported Maire, a distant cousin's daughter, to do the upstairs and perhaps wait on table. She ordered

Maire around as if she were a commanding general and Maire in her sixteen-year-old person an entire army with banners.

Down at the farm, chicks were started for the table. Mr. Pennyfeather, the estate manager, trembled as he tried to get the accounts straightened out, and wondered if Mr. Gordon would have a sharp eye for the rather ruthless cutting in the far plantations. But even Pennyfeather was caught up in the burst of activity in the last days: he brought over his men and had the windows washed.

"Glory be to God," said Annie as she came round the curve of the lower drive and saw the windows shining bright gold in the morning sun, the limestone face of the house like a sleeping beauty touched alive. "It's a great sight to be seeing in the morning, a grand house surely."

Sheltered by the frieze of trees, the ancient elephant hills behind it, Dene's Court relied on proportion alone: a high Italianate façade; of the twenty windows, those on the first floor were long, those on the upper two floors almost square. This façade without ornament, hardly broken by terrace steps and the high central door, was constantly changing in the changing light, a surface made to take the sun, to turn pale gold or dark slate under the influence of cloud or rain, making its only compromises with the weather. It *was* a grand house, grand in a plain enlightened way that spoke of the age in which it had been built. But it was in no sense charming, and to some eyes might even appear forbidding, rather too aloof, or even too exposed. It boasted of no gentle view of river or carefully planned opening perspective of trees or artificial lake. It faced the east and looked no further than the rough rolling Irish lawn which rose around it to form a bowl, enclosed in the trees at the edge of the demesne.

But for Annie it was too steeped in memories ever to be seen in this detached way. The drawing room furniture, the grand piano Violet's mother had played, and the great Aubusson carpet had been sold long ago: this part of the house was kept closed. Yet in spite of these attritions, and perhaps because it had not been lived in for so long, the house still held intact the atmosphere of all those summers when two sisters in white dresses had grown up, danced, run up and down the stairs, burst into tears, shouted with laughter. The high-ceilinged many-windowed rooms enclosed intense distilled life, and even grief now seemed as clear as drops of rain. So Annie felt, busily flinging windows open, leaning out of the master's bedroom to look down for a moment at Cammaert, bent over the lawn mower, giving the one piece of clipped English lawn to the right of the house a last grooming. Cammaert looked up on hearing the grinding of the window above him, and gave Annie a slow melancholy nod.

"It looks lovely!" Annie called down.

But he did not answer, only slowly shook his head and plodded on. "What with the slugs," he muttered to himself, "what with the rainy spring and the blight on the roses," and he sighed. "Miss Violet has no idea—

twenty years with no one but that rascal to look out for things. They'll have a shock. Neglect . . ." Cammaert sighed again. "I'm too old to do the work of four gardeners. What do they expect?"

Annie was too busy and happy to think such thoughts. She and Maire scoured and polished, sent for chimney sweepers, exhausted themselves dusting the books one by one, flapped blankets out of windows, shook out sheets to dry by the fires, and stopped every hour or so to drink innumerable cups of strong tea while Annie poured out stories of the Denes, and Maire listened, silent, her eyes wide. ("A deep one," Annie thought, "but teachable, tractable, and in fact," she decided with relief, "she'll do.")

As Annie talked on, processions of summers rose up and faded away; carriages gave way to motor cars; the tennis court was laid out; croquet parties came and went; Jonas Oliver Dene and his wife Elisabeth (Violet's grandparents) seemed always to be alighting from a drive and standing on the terrace steps waving at someone. Maire listened and later nodded to herself in the tarnished mirrors in the empty drawing room, trying to imagine the great beauty of Miss Violet, and the wildness of Miss Barbie. She passed the stables, overgrown with nettles and murmured, "Sixteen horses, Annie said, the carriage, the phaeton, the dogcart, the wagonette." Maire murmured as if she could conjure them up by naming them, for whatever did a phaeton look like? But that was in the grandparents' day, she remembered.

8

It was hard to keep it all straight in her head. "What was the footman's name?" she would ask, for she was fascinated by the idea of this man who wore a blue coat with silver buttons and whose only function was to get down and open and close the gates for the coachman to drive through. "Patrick, of course, was his name," Annie would say impatiently, as if she had forgotten one of the Kings of England.

And Maire imagined the servants' meals in the servants' hall when eight sat down to tea and the butler, a Protestant, Annie said, but a good sort, sat at the head. Maire's imagination was so full of all this that she felt she was walking about in a dream, and she half expected Miss Violet to drive up in a phaeton with a liveried footman and step out onto the terrace in a gauzy dress like a heroine in a musical. And what would Mr. Charles Gordon be like? Handsome, Annie said. But she didn't talk much of Mr. Gordon. She talked about the earlier past, about the long summers, about the two little girls, one beautiful, one mischievous.

On the last day Annie made a careful tour of the rooms, and was dismayed to realize for the first time how shabby everything was, how worn the carpets, how faded the curtains and walls; the bright light pouring in through the washed windows seemed a dangerous light. "For all we've done, it's going to be a sad home-coming." She sat down on a straight chair in the great front hall, now used as a dining room. She was suddenly exhausted to the marrow of her bones. For the first time the house bore down on her as a great empty weight, a shell. "We've done all we can," she said, feeling bitterly that it was not enough.

But just then Maire emerged from the back stairs and stood in the doorway, her arms full of flowers, roses and sweet peas and marigolds and bachelors' buttons. She stood there panting a little as if she were bringing an offering to a god.

"I've got them," she said as if the flowers were wild animals she had hunted down.

"Newspapers, you silly girl," Annie said crossly. "You'll make an awful mess otherwise. The jars are upstairs in the cupboard on the landing—you know where, don't you?—underneath."

But somehow the vision of Maire with her armful of flowers had brought back like a musical phrase the rich aura of all the summers. Annie got up, gave the long Sheraton table a final gloss, and began to sing as she worked. The great shell hummed faintly with the sound of distant seas, the rumor of the past that filled the silence and enclosed them in its spell. Annie looked up for a moment at the portraits of the Denes. They filled the high wall before her, their heavy gold frames gone dull against the faded apricot of the wallpaper (it had once been crimson). She could name them all from Cornelius Dene, the Colonel who had come over with Cromwell's armies, to Jonas Oliver Dene and his wife Elisabeth, Violet's grandparents. "The Denes," she said to herself, straightening up as if to receive an order for a dinner for twenty, "will be pleased."

But that night Violet Dene Gordon, surrounded by the safe Victorian comfort of a bedroom in the Shelbourne Hotel in Dublin, lay beside her husband and could not sleep. All through the last months she had felt the tug of Dene's Court like an obsession, had gone upstairs in the midst of a conversation to add an item to a list for Annie, and then sat forgetting why she had come, only wanting to think and remember, playing the past like a game of solitaire which must "come out," for if it did, all would be well with the future too. She set the small concrete details, names of flowers in the garden, children's books they had read with their father, Barbie's collections of insects and butterflies, set these out and looked at them with passionate attention as if they held the answer to huge questions and doubts. Would Charles really take hold and be happy there? Or would he be bored?

It was no joke for any man to be on the loose in his early fifties, cut off from the job for which he had been trained, to come back then to an England so changed that even in Lady Somerset's house, where there was still a butler, the guests helped wash the dishes. Their English friends teased them about the luck of being Anglo-Irish in these times. "You can get servants, I'm told," Lady Somerset said, "I'm mad with envy," and her husband added "meat" (looking rather like a cannibal, Violet thought). It was queer to feel oneself so naked, so orphaned, so cut off and yet in the eyes of one's friends to appear as the inheritors of a stability which hardly seemed possible any more. So it had always been with Dene's Court which had escaped burning when other houses of its kind were burned, which had stood since its building in a kind of aloofness which now appeared to be strength, some secret power of reserve, but was more likely luck, Violet thought—a matter of location, far from the centers of revolution and passion. For Violet suspected that the Denes had been neither better nor worse than other landlords.

Landlord. The word frightened her. It was as if she and Charles were asked to be fully grown-up for the first time in their lives. It suggested masses of children and servants. Children they did not have; Violet had never ceased to feel sorrow and guilt because of her miscarriage and the subsequent operation which destroyed all their hopes. Now in relation to the house, she felt the loss again and in a new way. She was not only failing Charles but all the Denes, coming back, barren, middle-aged, coming back as to a refuge to a house which had been designed not as a refuge at all,

12

but as a perhaps arrogant statement of faith in a way of life, in a tradition. Beside this their life in Burma had been improvised—that indeed was its charm. Now they would enter a more severe frame. Charles would sit at the head of the long table—so much too long for two— under the eyes of all the Denes.

So Violet had held back, persuaded him that they must have a few months of real holiday before taking on their new responsibilities. She had held back as one holds back from meeting an old love, because she was afraid, because too much was at stake.

Now on this last night the house rose before her closed eyes like a fortress, its twenty dark windows gleaming in the moonlight; behind it, the sheltering outlines of the mountains, milky above the intensely black trees. Moved passionately by this evocation, Violet turned toward her husband and laid her cheek against his back. She breathed in the steady pulse of his sleep and wondered what it would be like after this in the great fourposter bed where her parents and grandparents had slept in the peaceful summer nights. He did not move.

And suddenly Violet felt a longing for her sister, Barbie, for someone who would remember and share. She thought of their mother playing Chopin while they lay under the piano, rather frightened, for the reverberations suggested some great animal imprisoned there; she thought of Miss Goddard, their governess, taking them out to pick bluebells in the woods; of the long fierce games of croquet that lasted for days; of the rainy afternoons cutting out paper dolls. But she could not rest in these memories and turned over as if to ward off nightmare. For the peaceful summers had finally mounted in a crescendo through Barbie's violence, her escapes, her tantrums, her ambivalent feelings about this older sister who by her very presence had made Barbie feel deprived—till the final breaking off of everything and Barbie's departure for America with her husband. It was all so very long ago, yet the wounds had never been healed. The final memories of the house had been cruel, violent and were perhaps another unacknowledged reason for Violet's reluctance to go back.

There had been, after all, no reconciliation with Barbie, only the occasional letters at Christmas, the snapshots of Sally, Violet's niece whom she had never seen. Now that we are grown-up and getting old, Violet thought, if only we could talk—but Barbie had become efficient, was busy on all sort of committees with queer names (Americans organized everything so!). Violet suspected that if they did meet again Barbie would judge her severely, a beautiful woman who needed above all to be admired. Barbie would judge her marriage, would judge Charles (Americans never understood the British). It might in fact be quite unbearable and Violet, who had a moment before longed for her sister, quietly closed her mind. One can't go back, she thought—and then lay, rigid with apprehension, realizing that going back was just what she would have to do tomorrow.

"Charles!" She said sharply aloud, as if someone had knocked.

Charles turned in his sleep, groaned, and then sat straight up in bed, wide awake, cross. "What is it, Violet? What's the matter?"

"I'm sorry, darling—a bad dream, I guess. Go back to sleep." She folded her hand into his, as if she could lock away her anxiety there. And indeed she felt drowsy at last, as if their enfolded hands became an entity. "I could never do it alone," she thought.

At noon the next day in the steady fine rain, Cammaert puttered about transplanting petunias to the borders near the house, but stopped so often to listen for the gate at the upper drive, and relit his pipe so many times that he did not get much work done. "Damn the rain," he muttered. His feet were wet through, and he felt so angry with impatience he would have liked to kill something and stamped with satisfaction on a slug. Poor Maire down in the kitchen was near to tears, the butt of Annie's nerves. First there was the rain—and a flare-up of Annie's rheumatism so she felt clumsy and angry too:

the cream wouldn't whip; she burned her fingers on the oven as she put the roast in. Nothing could go right that morning cruel with suspense.

"Run along now and see if they're not coming," Annie said to Maire for the fifth time, "and this time don't come back till you hear the gate click—though how you'll hear it in this rain God only knows. Give a call-out," she followed Maire to the foot of the stairs and reminded her.

Maire, silent with emotion, went slowly up the stairs, through the hall and put her head out onto the terrace and listened. But all she could hear was the water in the gutters, a steady trickle from leaves, and somewhere near-by some little bird chirping. She was filled with foreboding, had visions of the car turned over in a ditch on some faraway road and Miss Violet and Mr. Charles Gordon bloody and quite dead. And whatever would we do then, she thought—indulging herself in this imaginary woe so that the tears she had held back all morning stood in her eyes, for the sheer pity of all she could imagine, and the relief of something definite and final after the weeks, the days and now the morning of intolerable suspense.

But in the midst of this the grind and clang came through the air as sharp as a dog's bark. It must be they —but what if it weren't and she called Annie for nothing? She waited for what seemed an eternity and heard the sound again and then ran, shouting at the top of her voice which had not made a sound all that day,

"Annie, Annie, it's them!" terrified by her own cry and the panic in it.

Annie charged past, pulling a coat over her head. "Don't stand there gaping, you silly girl. Put more coal on the fire in the library and then come out and help bring in the bags."

Violet and Charles saw the odd flapping figure emerge onto the terrace as they came out from under the trees in the little black Austin. "Thank God, it's Annie," Violet murmured. "She's here." They had no time to look up, to take in the bleak rainy face of the house. Violet was being hugged like a child. "Welcome home, Miss Violet, doatie—God be praised."

"Well, Annie, do you remember me?" Charles shook her hand warmly. "It's been a long time."

"And this must be Maire," Violet was saying, quick to take in the poor girl's scared face, her half-curtsy. "Be a good girl and help Mr. Gordon with the bags . . ." and she pulled Annie up the steps and into the great hall, for now she couldn't wait another second to go in, to take possession. "Wouldn't it be a day like this, Annie? Wouldn't it just?" she said flinging her tweed coat down, tearing off her rubbers with one quick gesture.

"Have we ever arrived when it didn't rain?" she asked, moving around, flying from this to that as if her agitation made an aura of wings around her and she was beating them, trying to settle, glancing up at the wall of portraits, taking in the polished surface of the dear beautiful table with a quick affectionate gesture of one hand, then turning to Annie, coming to rest at last as she looked at Annie, gaunt, fierce as ever with the same wisps of white hair escaping the tight knot at the top of her head, the same deep-set penetrating blue eyes, while all the rest of her, petticoat showing as always, was never quite set aright, as if she lived in a perpetual gale.

"Dear Annie, you haven't changed—not a bit," Violet said. "You're not a day older."

Annie tossed her head. "A scarecrow like me never grows old," and suddenly she laughed aloud at her own joke, "except for my rheumatic knee, a devil of a thing . . ." she added and then stopped as she looked for the first time at Violet.

Violet read in those honest eyes all Annie didn't say. "I've changed, Annie—isn't it awful? But you know it's been a long time, and I feel old—"

"Nonsense," Annie said shortly. "Yourself will always be a beauty, that's sure."

But Violet felt it suddenly unbearable to have Annie see the twenty years on her face, as if she had been found out. She ran into the library to look for Charles, calling,

"Oh Charles, leave the bags. Come and sit down. We're home!" But there was no answer. She went to the immensely high window to look out and saw Charles, oblivious of the rain, talking to Cammaert, their two heads close together, nodding. Cammaert lifted his hat, as if he were saying good morning and she had never been away at all.

She struggled to open the window, then gave it up and instead ran out bareheaded in the rain, for she must know what they were discussing so earnestly, she must be part of it all.

"It's the slugs," Cammaert explained, "as I'm telling Mr. Gordon, the garden is a ruin. It's the damp—" the old voice repeated as it had done in just the same words when she and Barbie used to burst into giggles at this unchanging litany of woe.

"There must be a blight on the roses," Violet murmured mischievously.

"Aye," Cammaert launched happily into the blight. But he was not allowed to finish. Charles, slipping an arm through his wife's, pulled her away. "Darling, you can't stand here in this wet without a coat. I'll have to see if the gin's arrived all right. We must have a drink before lunch."

But before moving they turned and looked up together at the façade above them. From here at the foot of the terrace steps, it towered. The stone had turned a dark grey in the rain. There was no softness here, no yielding to softness.

"Does the house welcome us, I wonder?" Violet asked, holding Charles's arm very tightly.

"It had better or we'll have to take it by storm." He gave the dark windows a bold look, but did not smile; Violet broke away from him and ran in. She stood just inside the glass door at the threshold of the great hall. Annie and Maire had disappeared. Her eyes went from the rows of Dene faces on the high wall to her left, to the long shining empty table, and then up the wide flight of stairs at the far end of this room into which all the other rooms of the house poured, the center of movement, of all currents. One would have to be strong indeed not to feel unbearably exposed here.

Do we have enough life in us, she wondered, to fill these spaces? To withstand all this? Would their voices ever sound natural and not as if they were breaking a willed silence? Violet stood still and took a deep breath.

But even when they were sitting by the fire a half hour later, she kept having the sensation that they were talking above something, not a noise exactly, but a very loud silence, and she laughed more than she meant to as if she must underline her presence, not to be swallowed up by this other presence. The drink helped. Charles helped, quietly active, already opening the glass-doored Victorian bookcases to take out bound copies of Dickens and exclaim with pleasure. He could move freely about because he was not stopped at every step by memory. He could stand as he was doing now at her grandfather's desk without having to displace first the shadow of that monumental man who at any moment (so Violet felt) would turn and give a loud roar. Her grandfather's chief way of communicating with his little granddaughters had been to pretend to be a giant and give strange howls, and when they ran away to Miss Goddard screaming ostentatiously, he felt that he was a success as a grandfather, but to them he appeared not as a person at all, only some violent force of nature like a volcano which they could make erupt by tiptoeing into the library on Sunday morning. He died when Violet was six or seven so he had remained a blundering bogeyman to whom the little girl felt slightly superior.

But there was Charles, real, unaware, standing in the window, and Violet got up impulsively and drew him out to explore the house. "I can't wait another minute!" she cried. "We'll take our drinks and go exploring—"

"Lunch will be served," Charles protested. "There isn't time—"

"But I can't wait another minute," Violet repeated, feeling as his slightly irritated, amused glance rested on hers a second, that she was released into the real present again, drinking in his love so that it actually coursed through her like blood itself, reviving. She led him up the wide stairs where they sat for a moment on the window seat on the landing and peered out through the rain and the swaying tops of the trees and the grey mists which eclipsed the mountains. But Charles, to whom this view meant nothing since it was not there, was more interested in the portrait of Cromwell at the top of the last flight to the second floor.

"It's quite a good painting," she said, "isn't it, Charles? You know I never really looked at it before. It was just there . . ."

After the two landings, each as big as a room, the stairs simply disappeared, vanished.

"The money gave out," Violet explained. "There was

supposed to be another flight to the ballroom," and she pulled Charles through a narrow door into perfect darkness. "How strange," she said, "I can't remember where the light is." So it was Charles's lighter which showed them the way, past the one toilet in the house, and up a narrow dark stairway into the rather surprising long low room, extending the full width of the house, windowed at each end, which had been designed as a ballroom but never finished.

"This is where we played on rainy days—that trunk used to be filled with 'grandeurs' (that's what we called them) for dressing up," she explained. "We used to slide too and make an awful noise . . ."

But she could not wait, though Charles was anxious to look more closely at the plaster ceiling where someone had sketched in a design, but given up. She was pulling him to the bedroom at the right, which she explained had been her room, with Barbie across the hall, running over in her bare feet when there was a thunderstorm and flinging herself into Violet's bed like a small thunderbolt herself.

"What a formal room for a child," Charles exclaimed. "Didn't you feel lonely?"

"Oh no—" Violet had gone to the windows as one must always do first in this house. "Come here, Charles . . ." They stood for a moment looking up at the long rolling lawn that was not a lawn but just rough grass which the sheep kept down, at the carefully placed grove of oaks in the hollow to the left and then the slow rise to a frieze of trees, very green, very still, very self-enclosed. "Isn't it beautiful, Charles—even in the rain?"

And then they turned together and looked back into the room, suddenly warm, the crimson puff on the bed glowing, the little roses on the Victorian dresser with its jug and washbasin and slop basin, gleaming.

"When you first came, I looked down from here and saw you. Do you remember, Charles? You rode over from the Olivers'—poor dears, they're dead now . . ."

But Charles was not listening. He had gone back to the ballroom which fascinated him, and besides he was feeling hungry. Sensing this, Violet took him rapidly through the other rooms, Miss Goddard's at the back and one of the guest rooms. She didn't take him into Barbie's room—she hesitated just yet to go in there, to disturb the passionate ghost, to bring back even for a moment, those wild tears—not just yet, she thought, in the rain. It's too sad.

"I'm hungry," Charles announced. "Whatever is Annie doing?"

"Nothing's on time, here, darling—or rather it all has a time of its own. Come and see our room. I've saved it for last."

Their room was on the floor below, just under Violet's. At the door, Violet turned and hesitated. "I'm scared," she said, "are you?"

"Why?"

"Well," Violet suddenly felt shy of this husband she had lived with for thirty years, "this is the room we do

23

have to take by storm," and quickly she flung open the door before these words should have an echo from the past.

There it stood, the great bed, so high that Violet as a little girl remembered sliding off when she tried to climb up on it. The faded yellow brocade of the canopy and spread had turned now a beautiful dull gold. On the dressing table Maire had put a bunch of syringa and yellow roses in the Venetian glass flecked with gold which Violet's mother had loved. The room seemed very high and airy and cool. Objects here kept their distance from each other, the dressing table across one corner, the chaise longue lying against the window that faced the formal lawn. There was no crowding possible. Their trunks, the pile of coats on the bed, the open suitcase on a stand, were absorbed in its spaciousness, and now its spaciousness seemed inhabited by the rain. It was a corner room so that the weather could not be shut out—involuntarily Violet shivered, and crossed the room to explore Charles's dressing room behind it, with the queerest sensation that her father must be there, and would fleck soap with his shaving brush at her. Instead it looked empty. The Victorian armoire gave a loud creak as she opened the door to peer inside.

For the first time Charles was troubled by the intangible presences here. For this was the heart of the house, the place where its secret life had been lived for generations. He felt its exposure: from within, the freight of memories; from without, the inescapable invading light or dark, sun or rain through the big naked windows.

He waited for Violet to come back, with something like anxiety as if she might from moment to moment change, be wholly absorbed by these presences he could not see but felt through her. She had stayed in the dressing room only a second but as she came back Charles was waiting for her at the door and took her almost roughly into his arms, as if he were taking her from a rival.

Violet, unprepared for this, coming back to him from under the wave of the past, met the change of focus in his eyes, the self-enclosed obsessive look which did not see her at all. Never would she yield to it without a moment of tremor, of fear, of almost withdrawal, for it meant yielding up her private self. As if to hold back this impersonal force in him, she laid a hand on his cheek very gently and felt the shape of the bone there. But to Charles this light, so personal touch came as an electric shock. He broke away and said gruffly, "We really must go down."

"Yes, darling," she said, letting her hand absent-mindedly slip along the bed as they passed. Then she closed the door gently upon all the lovers. It was an immense relief to know that they would come back here now to find themselves, would come back already to their own past.

"She seems awfully old," Maire said tactlessly when she and Annie sat down to a cup of tea before doing the dishes.

"Old indeed?" Annie looked at this baby with withering scorn. "To you maybe, who's barely out of the cradle —she's not more than fifty," Annie sniffed. "Twenty or more years younger than me, you'll be driving me to my grave, Maire, if you call the likes of her old."

"I just meant . . ." Maire was overwhelmed by Annie's capacity for speech, being herself a slow thinker with her tongue. She could go no further.

"And what did you mean?" Annie said crisply, loyalty bristling in her.

"Well—I thought you said she was beautiful . . ." Maire said, hanging her head for she well knew she was raising a storm.

But Annie was apt to do the unexpected. She was too strong a nature to have taken on the rigid mannerisms of what we like to call "a character." She did not fly out at Maire. She drank her tea and only after quite a time, she spoke softly, "It's a hard thing for her."

"But Mr. Gordon—he's handsome," Maire said anxious to make amends.

Annie sniffed. "Handsome is as handsome does," she said shortly. Annie would never admit that anyone who married a Dene was quite worthy, and she resented the fact that Charles did not show his age. She washed the dishes in silence, handing them over to Maire mechanically and thinking that it was queer to feel so weak in the knees, and that perhaps she should have a little nap before tea. After all she had hardly slept a wink with all the excitement.

Maire kept her thoughts to herself and was not perhaps aware of how quickly they changed, how quickly she forgot that first impression, which had been caused no doubt by the shock of a real person's coming between her and Annie's legends and her own dreams. Violet was not of course beautiful with the changeless white and gold beauty of a princess in a fairy tale as she had become in Maire's imagination. But she was still beautiful in more human terms.

This Maire felt when she brought in the breakfast tray the next morning and met for the first time, straight on, Violet's clear blue gaze. Had anyone ever not been melted by it?

"Good morning, Maire," Violet said, smiling a welcome to the shy girl whose hands always seemed to tremble when she was carrying anything. "What a lovely day after the rain!"

There was something about this voice too which troubled Maire though she did not know what it was, as if very simple things sounded like poetry. She did not dare raise her eyes again—they rested on the slim nervous ringed hands, and Maire thought without resentment, "What it is to be a lady and have such smooth hands."

There was something about the atmosphere of this room, the bottles of perfume on the dresser, the soft blue velvet wrapper flung down on the chaise longue, which filled Maire with excitement and devotion. So many impressions crowded in on her all at once that she was dismayed to find she hadn't heard Violet's question. It came to her after a second of silence. "Did Mr. Gordon have a good breakfast?"

"Oh yes," Maire said blushing, "very good."

"And he's gone out, has he?" Violet asked.

But when Maire had answered that Mr. Gordon had gone over to the farm to see Mr. Pennyfeather, she did not know how to get out of the room, and stood there, her hands at her sides, mortally embarrassed. Only when Violet noticed this and suggested that she might go now, did she run out, as if she had been released from a spell.

Violet would have liked to lie there for half the morning, not do anything except feel, soak in the peace—the wonderful peace of having arrived with Charles, of having really reached home. It was strange to think that even after thirty years of marriage such tensions could build up around the hours of passionate love and acceptance of each other. The months in England had been such a period of tension when Violet was forced to face the fact that she and Charles were not good friends; at such times they rubbed each other the wrong way and concealed their mutual irritation under a façade of extreme politeness, concern about health.

"You must have a good long rest after lunch, Violet," Charles would say, knowing or not knowing (Violet could never make up her mind which) that this meant that she was looking tired, knowing or not knowing that it had a concealed barb in it. And feeling diminished, looking at herself too much, too often in the mirror, she had to find a more flattering reflection in someone's eyes—and despised herself for it. At such times she envied plain acquaintances whose marriages had lapsed into nothing more than a steady taking-for-granted kind of companionship. No, her marriage had never ceased to be perilous, demanding, disappointing, ecstatic. It ebbed and flowed on its own secret tides and she wondered now sometimes what would happen when the tide ebbed for good. Like a poet who thinks in each dry period that he will never again be visited by the angels, Violet during each of these periods suffered a kind of terror and despair. It was necessary to maintain, to create the physical tension between them—without it, the meaning would go out of their mode of communication which was to be almost deliberately casual, flat. Charles could never express himself in words; and she did not wish to. Their flirtations with people outside this magnetic circle had never been serious and had perhaps been necessary.

Violet would have liked to lie in bed all morning thinking of these things, but the curtains had been pulled back and the brilliant daylight poured in on her, dazzling her eyes, making its imperative demands. Personal life which had always been intense in this house (so Violet guessed) partly by reason of its isolation, personal life must be framed in a ritual, a discipline. By nature she had always known this; here in the house what she knew instinctively was borne out concretely in every detail. Emotion must be concentrated or it would just vanish into the high empty spaces. This was not a room designed for daydreaming, a cosy boudoir. It took on its beauty by candlelight, and its greatness when the shutters were opened, the candles snuffed, and the small currents of wind and the great still spaces of the night free to take possession.

So Violet pushed the tray away and got up and went to close the windows, and to look out. That was the first part of the ritual—one must look out and discover the day. Now the grass was still wet with dew under the oak grove and the greenness seemed to shine. She met the blue sky full on with a shock of pleasure, for here a blue sky was always diaphanous, never flat, but radiant as if light poured through it. She had not at first noticed Charles but now he emerged from the plantation of trees at the top of the hill, hands in his pockets, Pennyfeather walking at a little distance behind him.

Violet could tell by Charles's stance that he was being authoritative and that he was not pleased, and she smiled. Then as he glanced down at the house, she leaned out to wave, and he waved back and she could sense his smile of pleasure in the air between them and the thread of their union pulled taut. A person always would give this landscape a peculiar poignance, she thought. A person looked so small, yet gave the spacious scene its necessary focus. How lonely, it must have felt here, she thought, all these years.

There was so much to be done, so much, that Violet hardly stopped at the dressing table, but dressed with nervous impatience, finding her brogues at the bottom of the shoebag and a heathery tweed skirt and sweater, then at the door turned back and put on her pearl earrings and a pearl necklace. She could not meet this day when the rituals would be established less than formally.

First she had a long talk with Annie in the kitchen while Maire did the upstairs. It began as a serious talk about meals, expenses, what they might count on from the farm, how often meat was delivered and so on. Violet had been prepared for the fact that Annie would know best, would as a last resort call up the shades of parents and grandparents to defend the boiled potato or vegetable marrow as the almost unique vegetable. Some things would have to be accomplished gradually and only by the use of tact amounting to genius. And Violet was prepared to take her time, so she agreed with almost all of Annie's suggestions and plans, especially as they were both eager to get business out of the way.

"Now you'll have a cup of tea," Annie said firmly, and that meant, Violet knew, a heart to heart talk.

"The dear kitchen, Annie—the smell of it . . ." she sighed. It was the smell of onions and mint and tea, and a general spicy smell which came from the little spice cupboard to the left of the stove; this mixed with wood burning and the sharp dank taste of coal in your mouth, and of damp dishcloths drying out on a rack.

"I don't know as we'll ever get the laundry free of the damp," Annie was saying. "The walls were mildewed. And what with all the rest, I've hardly had time to dry it out."

"You've done wonders, Annie. I don't know how—"

"Well, it was high time you came back, Miss Violet, I'll say that. I'm telling you I was all of a tremble when I put the key in the lock the first time—the emptiness of it, Miss Violet! It was enough to scare the heart out of you." Annie shook her head, then looked across at Violet and smiled her rare smile. "But in no time, what with the fires and the open windows it began to feel like itself."

"It's strange isn't it, Annie, how it never changes— only we've changed. The house is the same," Violet said in her musical voice, for she was Irish enough to enjoy the melancholy of this.

"You always did talk nonsense in such a way that the angels themselves would imagine you spoke the truth," Annie said roughly. And Violet laughed, "Oh Annie it's good to be home!"

"That's more like it." Then as Violet got up to go

Annie threw in casually, "I wouldn't be surprised now if Miss Barbie took it into her head to come over one of these days—"

"I'd be very much surprised," Violet said quietly and turned away. She did not want to think of Barbie just now, just yet.

No, this first day must be carefully designed. Later, supported by the design, she could afford to remember the difficult, the painful things. Not now, not yet.

So she slowly climbed up the back stairs, without hurrying, and out into the brilliant sunshine that flooded the hall and showed up rather cruelly the faded wallpaper, torn strips hanging down at the far end— Charles must see to that, Violet noted.

She stood with the long table between her and the portrait-covered wall and looked for a moment at the gathered Denes, one by one. They were all there except her father and mother, dressed in brocade and satin, looking down at her without surprise, without condemnation, accepting her as she accepted them—even Great-Aunt Sarah St. Leger, the one exaltée of the lot, for she had been so altered in mind by the horrors of the Famine that she had devoted the rest of her life to good works. The Dene attitude toward this aunt could be summed up in something Violet had heard her gentle unworldly father say with a sigh, "Yes, Sarah," he had said, "no doubt she hoped that someday one of us would follow in her footsteps. But I fear she was the exception that proves the rule."

"What's the rule, Father?" Barbie had asked. They

were standing just where Violet stood there and, she remembered, it was raining and the plan to pick mushrooms had had to be abandoned for fear Barbie would catch a cold.

"Oh, I don't know," he said, playing with the ring on his little finger as he did when he was faintly embarrassed, "something about a pattern of life carried on through the generations. Sarah St. Leger was outside the pattern. Possibly she had greatness so the pattern constricted her. But to some of us," he added half to himself, "it has meant a kind of freedom. For the matter of that, we're all eccentrics," he said, patting Barbie's little dark head.

"Violet isn't," Barbie said with scorn. "She just wants to be liked."

And he had laughed, "Yes, I doubt if Great-Aunt Sarah would approve of Violet."

But Violet knew by the way her father looked at her that he did approve, so it didn't matter about that old Aunt.

Did it matter now, since this scene so long ago had come back so vividly to her mind? Or had it after all mattered then, mattered so much that she had buried it and never thought of it again?

No, said Violet, looking up at the small aloof erect head on the wall, dark hair falling in ringlets and deep red evening dress (for this portrait had been painted before Great-Aunt Sarah's devotion to the poor and sick had been unlocked). No, Violet said to herself, our life, Charles's and mine, has not been meaningless. If she thinks so, she's quite wrong. Nor for that matter, had their father's—unlucky, impractical though it was. Dene's Court had lost some of its grandeur in the days of her father, but what did that count beside his gentleness, his quiet wisdom, his patient botanical studies? His entire lack of business acumen—what did that matter beside what he was as a person?

And now, Violet thought, as if she had been interrupted unkindly, I really must get out and find Cammaert. Leaving the house, going out into the cool fair June day, she felt her heart lift with almost aching delight. It came over her in waves that she was really going to live here, that they would not have to leave it again, that she would for the first time in her life see every season in the house, in the woods, across the rough flung carpet of the lawn. The rising up of the rooks in battalion in September would not be the sign that they too must rise and go.

Cammaert was busy with the petunias in the parterres in front, but he was only too glad to lead her through the familiar green tunnel, past the stables overgrown with nettles, along by the brook and finally along the high brick wall to the gate of the big garden. Violet was accompanied every step of the way by memories of her mother who had done this every fair morning when she was well enough, always stopping to listen to the brook, always eager with anticipation, walking too fast for the little girls behind her and then swooping down upon them with a smell of verveine which she got from Floris in London, a white Chinese shawl flung round her

shoulders and the long fringe getting caught in the bar-
rettes of the little girls' hair. They had reached the gate
long before Violet had finished with all that flowed
down the brook to her, and now she stood hesitating,
while the vision of the glorious rather stiff set pieces
her mother spent hours arranging came before her eyes,
and she was conscious, holding the flat basket her
mother had carried, that she was about to pick up and
continue a musical phrase. Where it had all stopped, it
would begin again, and the empty basket be filled. Cammaert was holding the gate open for her—would it all
be changed?

The paths needed scraping; there were, she noticed,
breaks in the wall in two places (the work of hard frost
no doubt); the little arbor where her mother often sat
embroidering, sheltered here from the wind, had quite
fallen in. But the three benches surrounding the sundial, rusty and in need of paint, were still there. And
above all, the smell was still there—Violet ran to press
rose geranium and lemon verbena between her fingers.
And then she felt ready to face Cammaert and to go
with him slowly from rose to rose, listening to the
pent-up tales of the years, of the awful drought which
had killed some of the espaliered peach trees against the
south wall, of rainy summers which had brought blight
and mildew, of frosts which had cracked the wall open
and ruined one parterre of what Cammaert called "new-
fangled roses." While he talked Violet listened and con-
doned and above all looked around, shading her eyes

36

from the sun, regretting that she had not worn a hat. The garden had always looked as it did now, half-finished, a little ragged, with the parterres of picking flowers at one end and the vegetables and the rows of sweet peas fencing this part off from the center round the sundial where an attempt had been made at a formal French garden, though the box had died years ago so the edges looked crumbly. It had always been a place of struggle, full of dreams of things which never got done —— Her grandfather had wanted a fountain. Her mother spent days in bed making lists, surrounded with catalogues. It had always had an unfinished look, yet in those days there had been three gardeners. Violet realized for the first time what it had meant to work here alone, the long often hopeless battle.

"We'll never be able to thank you, Cammaert," she said, laying a hand gently on his unyielding stiff old arm. "But it looks beautiful," she shouted, wondering how much he heard, "I'll start picking tomorrow." But he had turned away with a grunt, and was busily cleaning aphis off a rose.

His love for the gardens was, she thought, like an illness, a despairing love, never satisfied, intensely self-critical, with apparently no joy in it. But it had instead a kind of greatness. It was selfless. It did not even need her praise, or only as she was part of a whole which was by no means altogether composed of human beings.

"I wonder, Charles," she said, as they sat in the library drinking martinis before lunch, grateful for the coolness here after the hot sun, "can we ever give them the support they have given us—Annie, Cammaert—can we ever serve in the way they have served?"

"Pennyfeather's been lining his own pockets, I can tell you," Charles said cutting through her tone deliberately.

"Oh well, he's not one of us. It's business with him" —Violet was scornful of this manager imported from England—"What did you expect?"

"The accounts are in the most awful mess. I'll have my hands full," Charles said cheerfully. He liked nothing better than a challenge of this sort. He swelled like a pigeon with pleasure.

"You'll do very well as a country squire, darling," Violet said demurely.

But Charles did not rise to this barb. He was wholly absorbed in his morning's discoveries. He walked up and down talking of the need for new plantations ("that rascal has been cutting and selling, I'll wager"), lamenting their lack of capital ("the farm needs new stock badly but we'll have to wait") while Violet, half listening, drank her martini and breathed in the peace.

"These chairs really do need recovering," she said aloud.

"You're not listening," Charles said crossly.

"I'm sorry—what was it, darling?"

"Never mind." Then they laughed. It was such a familiar pattern. "Have you had a good morning?" Charles asked and it meant, "I love you, even though you never listen to what I say."

The clock on the stairs struck one as if to frame the moment. After Violet's answer, they sat silent, looking at the fire.

After lunch Violet rested for an hour, glad to be alone in the bedroom, not closing the shutters so that she felt bathed in sunlight and in silence, half-awake with the sense of layers and layers of summers, generations of summers coming alive just by the fact of one person being here, one person holding the so slight, so perilous thread of the past in her consciousness. But after me, Violet thought, after Annie and Cammaert—what then? And because it was a dying splendor they could still keep alive for a few years, it seemed even more vivid and dear, requiring more of them than of other Denes who had taken for granted, perhaps, what they would consciously hold and sustain against the uncertain changeable future. Violet felt deeply excited.

After tea, at Annie's suggestion, Charles drove her down to the village to see Mrs. O'Connell and the clerk at the post office and the grocer, but everyone they met spoke to them and welcomed them.

"I feel like the Prince Consort," Charles said on the way back. "But won't the Vicar be offended?" he teased. "We forgot to call on him."

"I expect he will." Violet was dismayed. "Oh dear . . ."

Charles had meant it as a joke and told her not to take herself too seriously, but Violet only felt and was absorbed in the intense pleasure of coming back to the house for the first time.

Charles did not want to dress for dinner, but to Violet this was a matter of crucial importance. It was the final piece of the pattern which she had been creating all day. When she came down the great staircase in her smoky grey velvet dress, a rose pinned at the throat (she had bought this dress in London and kept it on purpose to wear this first evening) and found Charles, all black and white, standing in front of the fire in the library, she felt like a captain bringing his ship in to a perilous landing.

"Wherever did you get that dress, darling? You look absolutely marvelous . . ."

"And the house, Charles," Violet said quickly, looking at the firelight reflected in the glass doors of the bookcase across the room, and out through the long windows at the intensely green twilight through the leaves, at the rather quaint fat bunch of pink roses on the table facing the fire, the brown velvet sofa standing back to it, and then finally at the portrait of her father in the corner to the left, "Doesn't the house look different too at night?"

"Hadn't noticed," Charles said, for he was looking at her, "but now that you mention it, yes, the house has an air about it at night—I see what you mean about dressing for dinner. It sort of asks for it, doesn't it?"

"It's going to be all right, isn't it?" It was the question Violet had held back all day, feeling that it would be tempting fate to ask it, at least until the circle of this first day was closed and they were safe.

"Rather—" Charles was very busy about something at the little table where the drinks and glasses were kept. Now there was a loud pop followed by Violet's astonished cry.

"Champagne! Really, darling, can we afford it?"

"Of course we can't afford it. Here," and he held out to her one of the Venetian champagne glasses her grandfather had brought back from his Grand Tour. "It's not really cold enough, I'm afraid . . ."

"Oh Charles, do you remember, we had champagne for our engagement?"

"Of course I remember. You aren't the only one who has a past bound up in this house. On that occasion your father said, 'Bring her back someday, Charles.'"

The first week was a honeymoon. Both Charles and Violet felt the relief of not being guests any more and of making their way back into their own life. Every afternoon now after tea they went for a walk or took the car and went exploring or to the town some fifteen miles away to shop. They paid a few calls, though this house was so isolated that there were no "dropping-in" neighbors; in the evenings they took up their old habit of playing chess or Charles read aloud, for he laughed so much as he reread *The Pickwick Papers* that Violet begged him to share the joke. There were long comfortable silences when the clock on the landing ticked loudly and the fire stirred, or outside an owl cried. Violet who had feared that they would feel too isolated was surprised to discover that she had no desire to invite people, that in fact the silences were what she had been hungry for—time to think and feel and put down roots. One did not feel so much the passing of time as a kind of timelessness, the warm sun in the enclosed garden in the morning, the hum of bees, and the long slow twilights, the waking every morning to the weather, and the adjustment of the day to this chiefest presence.

It was at the same time a period of intense activity. Charles tramped for miles, marking trees to be cut or places which needed replanting, going out even when it rained, gradually coming to know far better than Violet herself did, every corner of the demesne, and the farm. He took over the offices which Violet's grandfather had had built in the new wing at the back of the house, cleaned out the piles of old papers and settled in there, ordering books on agriculture and forestry from London. Charles began to think that a change of profession was not at all a bad thing for a man of fifty. He felt ten years younger already he told Violet, and Violet who had always feared that if they were alone together, they would irritate each other, or that Charles would be bored, began slowly to relax.

Only, being a woman, she had moments of anxiety as she looked forward. Would it last? Wasn't so much quiet happiness something to be feared, a little gift to help them start along the new ways, but sure to be dissipated by—for instance—a long spell of bad weather, or the inevitable lag that would come when Charles saw his fine plans delayed by the human character of those he had to work with? What of the winter, Violet sometimes asked herself at the low ebb of the day when she was lying on the chaise longue? Cold would drive them inward and cut down the spaciousness of life. They would have eventually to put in central heating—and perhaps this first winter move to Dublin for a couple of months. It would be all right, she told herself, drowsily looking at the slanting light across the faded wallpaper, because . . .

Because, love. In Burma they had had the habit of reading in bed, under the white tent of mosquito netting; here, any light attracted moths (which Violet hated above anything) and even birds, so when they went to bed, they lay in the dark, windows wide open to the night, and this—or was it some powerful atmosphere belonging to the room itself?—bore them through the first week on a high tide of passionate response to each other. They were, through these first days, above all lovers. And every moment of the day rose toward the next night, and the next—I wonder if other middle-aged people have this experience, Violet thought. It seemed almost like a miracle, the proof of some deep renewal in themselves. Violet forgot to notice the fine lines round her eyes, to question her face each morning as if to read there the inexorable grain by grain passing of time; she read in Charles's eyes all she needed to know.

Yet there was a vital difference in this experience for her and for him. He did not constantly bump into the past, or edge away from memories which threatened or demanded. He did not have to catch his breath as he opened a door, or pause lost in thought on the landing as the blue mountains showed themselves on a fine day. He was not the center as she was of a fine but tightly drawn web of faces and feelings, and Violet sometimes felt she was living several lives at once. In her dreams they interwove themselves so she often woke confused, wondering who she was, surprised to find Charles beside her, surprised not to be woken by Miss Goddard's crisp "Time to get up, lazybones!"

Charles on the other hand was fascinated to know more of the history of the house. It was not the immediate past that held him but the early days. He hunted about in old drawers and cupboards while Violet rested, to try to find architect's plans of the house. He didn't find them, but he found other things, records of the Irish Volunteers to which an eighteenth century Oliver Dene had belonged, a rather dull journal which recounted visitors galore and games of cards and outings. The Denes had never it seemed been given to literary introspection.

"They were too busy living," Violet said, "and besides personal life didn't seem so all-important in those days—what people felt—"

"They took such things for granted you mean? Yes, I daresay they did, at that. But they read. There's a Montaigne in the library with old Colonel Dene's name in it."

Violet was quite amazed at how much Charles was able to reconstruct, how observant he was. Things she had always taken for granted and never questioned, bothered him. It was he who pointed out that her grandfather's authoritarian hand was visible all over the place —it was he surely who had invested in the solid Victorian furniture in the damp dining room, now unused in the closed part of the house. It was surely he who had built in the glass-doored box that kept drafts out from the hall, an architectural calamity but so necessary for comfort that it really couldn't be changed. It was he who had built the offices at the back, he the only practical Dene for three generations.

"You see," Violet explained, "he died when I was seven. Then for years it was grandmother who reigned here. Oh, Charles, you would have loved her. She used to ride all over the place in a pony cart, pointing out weeds with her whip handle and making George get down and pull them up there and then. She was very small and light on her feet, given to sudden tempers when her little round face would go quite pink. Barbie was terrified of her and had to be dragged to say good morning and turned her face away when Grandmother bent down to kiss her—but I loved her because she always treated me as a grown-up person."

Charles listened and pieced the past together. He had himself been brought up in India and then sent away to school. He had never known this sort of life, easy-going, planted on ancestral land. He found himself considering it objectively, weighing its purpose, its responsibilities, wondering about it.

"Why wasn't this house burned?" he asked one day. "I gather the Anglo-Irish had a bad time of it."

"Well," Violet had never asked herself this question. "Maybe it was too isolated—I think father said it was attacked once and barricaded just in time, but no one

46

was hurt. Whoever it was who threatened us went away after firing a few shots."

"Darling, how wonderfully vague you are!" Charles chuckled.

"Well, we just lived here, don't you see? Nobody told us the story as if it were a story, the way you look at it," Violet was nettled.

"It has," Charles said thoughtfully, smoking his pipe, "a monumental indifference to everything outside the demesne, and I expect that saved it, in the long run."

"You'll never understand, Charles. You're so British. None of this history is reasonable." Violet was quite cross now. She never called Charles British, setting herself apart as Anglo-Irish unless she was very cross. The years in Burma had diminished this racial difference which she had felt strongly at first. Now, coming back, the Irish in her was coming to the surface.

But Charles let it pass and went back to their chess game, which this conversation had interrupted. Only he took a certain pleasure in checkmating her more quickly and cruelly than usual.

"That for the Anglo-Irish," he said, teasing her and smiling broadly in his triumph.

But Violet's mood had changed. She lit a cigarette and puffed a few minutes in silence while Charles put more coal on the fire.

"It is a queer thing to be," she said, "neither one thing nor the other—very few of us ever bridge the gap. Maybe my great-great-aunt Sarah St. Leger did because

47

in a way she gave up being herself, went and lived in a cottage (I showed it to you the other day)—"

"Yes," Charles said, "I remember. She was the one who devoted herself to the poor people during the Famine."

"She was a saint, I suppose, and saints can do it, though they make everyone uncomfortable in the process."

"I take it she wasn't popular with the Denes."

"Well, 'enthusiasm' wasn't very popular with us at any time," Violet said unconscious of the we and all it implied.

Charles stood back to the fire, smoking his pipe, thoughtfully. "Still," he said after thinking this over, "there is a streak of it, isn't there? Your grandfather— he had a streak of it applied to business and the estate itself. He treated it all rather like a God-given task, is my guess." Charles chuckled. "My image of him is giving orders about pigs and corn rather like an Old Testament Prophet. To disagree with him was to disagree with the Law, the Bible, God—or so he imagined."

Violet smiled. "Yes, all that's why we never felt him quite as one of us like Grannie. He was too efficient."

"Yet without him the estate would have gone to pieces and your father could never have devoted his life to botany. The enthusiasts as you call them included Sarah St. Leger and possibly the Dene who built the house, a little more grandly designed than he had money to carry out. It's one of the threads woven through the steady cumulative discipline of what you call 'just living'—isn't it?"

"And now," Violet said demurely, "there's you."

"Goodness, I'm not an enthusiast."

"Aren't you?"

"Of course not," Charles said crossly, and Violet smiled with pleasure in him. Charles had such a capacity for throwing himself whole into whatever he was doing. In Burma he had learned the language at once, had worked hard at Hindustani, could speak Malay and Chinese after two years. He knew more about village customs in the hill villages where he went to recruit labor than many Burmese themselves did. And now in just two weeks he was at home among the Denes as if he had lived here long ago. He had a speculative mind which nourished itself on information as others might nourish themselves on poetry. And Violet, looking at him now with admiration, thought that this quality in him, active yet thoughtful, was perfectly rendered by his rather square head, close-cropped grey hair that revealed an open brow, by his straight short nose and firm mouth. The years had refined this Roman head which might have grown heavy, if he had put on weight. Instead the fine lines round the eyes (deep-set, dark blue) and the tension of the cheekbone gave his face an air of achieved balance. He had always worn authority with a special human grace and this had not diminished. He was, she thought, with a tremor of excitement caused by their earlier tiff, a fearfully attractive being.

"I wonder," he said a little later, "if Barbie has any grandchildren if they will want to come back."

The current of emotion which was always present in the house now assailed Violet like a draft and she shivered and got up, breaking the moment of desperate nostalgia (for it was never less than painful to face their own lack of children) by saying,

"I bet they're enthusiasts." She could not keep the edge of bitterness out of her voice, and later she found she was wide awake. For the first time since their return the emptiness of the house, the stillness of the demesne, for there was hardly a breath of wind, attacked her, frightened her and was only dissipated by her extreme fatigue as the dawn came, and she slept a troubled sleep.

The next day it rained and the next and though the sky lightened a few times and the clouds rolled off to the tops of the mountains, they were blown back and the rain misted down for almost a week. Even Charles began to be irritable, to find excuses to get off to town.

(To buy rubber boots, wool socks, so he said, but Violet knew that it was to get away into some small cosy pub and talk with the men. She could hardly blame him.) Violet felt panic rising in her and took refuge two or three times a day in the kitchen to drink a cup of tea with Annie, and the silent Maire in whose eyes she read the growing devotion which could alone give her back a sense of identity. The kitchen—she had always felt this even as a little girl—was the root of the house. All branched up and outward from it, and if the fire went out there could be no hope at all. But Annie saw to it that the fire never went out and that there was always a kettle at the boil and she knew the way to cheer up Miss Violet was to talk about the old days and people the empty rooms with the laughter and parties and people.

Then there was the post which the young postman's boy brought up on a bicycle a little after eleven. This was the signal for Violet to get up and settle in the library to read her letters by the fire, and to answer them until lunch (for she had always been a lavish correspondent. One had to be to maintain relationships from such a distance as Burma or from this almost equally isolated world). On rainy days this rite replaced the other, of gathering and arranging flowers.

It was queer how she never saw a letter from America without trembling. So strong was the bond with her sister, a bond which all the years had neither pulled tighter into a real intimacy, or ever loosened even a fraction from its painful tension. She sat with the letter in her hands, aware that it was longer than usual, wondering what news it might bring.

When she had read it through, she lit a cigarette and went over to stand at her grandfather's desk looking out at the wet leaves of the oaks, at the long sweep of rough grass, misted over by the fine rain. She was so startled that she had no thoughts, only rather violent and disconnected feelings. For Barbie had asked her point-blank to take her daughter Sally in for the summer, had intimated that the sooner Violet answered the better, and that a cable would be welcome. It seemed that Sally was at all costs to be removed from an emotional situation which Barbie and her husband did not wish to precipitate any further: she had fallen in love with an actor, a nice enough boy, Barbie said, with a Texas oil fortune in the background, but simply not to be trusted, much too sophisticated for Sally and, she was convinced, not serious. Whereas Sally, it appeared, was not only serious but determined to marry him at once; was behaving very much as her mother had behaved thirty years before (though Barbie had forgotten this, perhaps), was defiant, tearful, said she hated her parents and meanwhile was doing very badly at college. "I can't pretend that I am asking an easy thing of you, Violet," the letter had ended. "Sally will not want to come and I have never talked to her much about the house, but if you and Charles could bear to have her for a month or two, it might make all the difference to her future happiness."

Violet's first reaction had been "No, we're hardly settled; we've got to have time; we can't be expected to take on another problem right now." Only her thoughts were not reasoned in this way, they were more violent. It looked like an invasion—an American girl, too, that seemed the last straw. And Barbie's daughter, obviously difficult, emotional, God knew what. No, thought Violet, looking out at the drifting clouds which now seemed really to be blowing over . . .

Then she thought, after all, it will fill the empty spaces. Here's a child we're being asked to take in. Also, Charles . . . Always it made things easier rather than more difficult if there were other people about in their marriage. Violet knew that they each in his own way, responded to a third person.

And finally she knew that whatever other reasons there might be, she would have to say yes to Barbie. There was too much guilt to make her ever again able to take a stand where Barbie was concerned.

She'll have my room, Violet thought, already filling it in her mind's eye with roses, already opening her heart to this niece she had never seen. She went upstairs to try to find snapshots in a trunk she had not yet unpacked. There Charles found her, sitting on the floor with papers and letters strewn all around her, and in her hand the photograph of a little dark girl in boy's clothes looking down from an apple tree like a mischievous elf.

"Whatever are you doing, Violet?" Charles was cross. "I've been looking for you everywhere. Didn't you hear me call?"

"Put out the light, Charles, before you open the shutters—there must be swarms of moths waiting to get in
already . . ."

Charles never would remember, she thought irritably.
But at last all was done, the closed room opened to the
moonlight outside, for at last the weather had turned,
and now outside the air was milky white, and as Violet
and Charles lay in bed and got accustomed to the dark,
it seemed to grow brighter and brighter; they could see
the wide path across the foot of the bed and against the
sharp white of the closed door. A light cool wind stirred
the curtains. All seemed so clear and wide-open, so spacious and exciting after the long nights of enclosing
rain that they were drawn irresistibly to the windows
to look out, to look down on the side of the real lawn,
at the still flower beds, at the roses gone black in the
moonlight and the blue-white petunias. On the road,
the moonlight fell like snow. They did not say a word,
but stood close together, Charles's arm resting lightly
on Violet's shoulders, tasting the peace, the assurance

that all was well, given back to them quite simply by the clearing sky.

Violet gave a little breathless scream and brushed the air to try to catch the moth which she had felt, horribly soft against her cheek, beating its wings. She fled back to bed. But Charles stood on at the window.

"What really happened about Barbie, Violet?"

It was his need to know the facts, now that they had come to their decision and sent the cable. Charles had not seemed at all disturbed at the prospect at first, but later in the evening Violet felt his slight stiffening at the idea of an American, and noticed that he was looking at the house with a newly critical eye, wishing they could repaper here or recover chairs there, as if it suddenly mattered. It seemed extraordinary that in all these years she had never told him the story. Perhaps until now it had not seemed relevant.

"Come back to bed, darling," she said. "It's a long story."

It was not, she found, an easy story to tell. It took too many words and she felt strangely that none of the words told the truth. What was the truth? Barbie was the younger sister of a beauty, that was the first, the crucial fact.

"Yes, I expect you put her in the shade," Charles said, rather smugly, running a finger down her nose and mouth and chin with possessive pride.

"No, Charles, don't." Violet wanted to be able to think clearly. It was not only that even as a little girl Violet had been quite aware that she could get what she wanted by being charming and even as a small child enjoyed her power over people, and wanted praise so much that it was easy for her to conform. It was also that Barbie, who saw her sister winning easily what she had to struggle to achieve, had a violent nonconformist temperament. "She was," Violet said, "the most ardent person I've ever known." If Barbie ran a race she stumbled and fell out of the fierce longing to win; she wanted things too much and frightened people by her intensity.

"In a queer way," Violet said, "she had no luck." And she explained this: their father had been too gentle, too oblique to understand Barbie's fierce temperament. He was a little afraid of her. Their mother, who did understand and could tame the passionate child, was so often away (for she had always been threatened with tuberculosis and spent years at various times in sanatoriums) and when she was at home, so frail, to be cherished and not disturbed, that she moved at a little distance from the center of their life, it seemed. And Violet could not help, however desperately she wanted to, because of Barbie's always ambivalent attitude toward her, and jealousy. "She would have been far happier sent away to school, but we could not afford that—so she wore us all out. There was never any peace for long. She would run away on the day of a birthday party, for instance, or burst into tears when we had guests, and she did have an awful temper. She was always being punished—"

"Were you so frightfully good yourself?" Charles asked, his sympathy for the moment with Barbie.

"Of course not, but I was more subtle—and then of course I was older." That meant that Barbie wore Violet's cast-off clothes, was not allowed to do things Violet could do, had to go to bed earlier, was perpetually being thwarted, so it seemed. These were the childhood days. Violet spoke of them quite lightly and objectively. But then she was silent. When Charles turned to see if she had fallen asleep in the middle of her story, he realized that she was finding it difficult to go on. Why open these old wounds now? So he gently suggested.

"Old wounds, Charles?" She sat up in bed, her arms clasped round her knees. "All these years I've never stopped somewhere down deep being conscious of Barbie, being anxious. It's never been over, Charles. Isn't it queer?"

Often and often Violet had lain awake turning over in her mind the question, was being beautiful always tied to a burden of guilt? For beauty such as she had been given, as in the old fairy tales, was both a charm and a curse. Too often what life had given her had been taken from someone else; she felt the responsibility now. As a young girl she had been only self-intoxicated, needing to feel her power, flirting unconsciously and consciously every moment of the day, expecting homage as a princess expects it, taking it as her due. Though she never thought it was taking anything from Barbie— Barbie, the wild child, long-legged, awkward, who hated party dresses and parties, who grew up so slowly and had only contempt for Violet's young men, took out her feelings by beating them at tennis, but then when tea

57

was served more likely than not disappeared. In those days girls of twelve and thirteen didn't ask to wear lipstick; Barbie had still had braids down her back at fifteen and wept angrily when she had to put them up the next year. It had all happened suddenly—overnight in fact—when that queer young man Philip Oliver turned up with his parents.

He looked like a small rather awkward robin, for he was short for his age, with a thatch of dark hair and very bright brown eyes, as bold and glancing as a bird's. He was eighteen but looked younger. Violet recognized him at once as a person like herself with a secret charm for whom doors would open wide. He was bubbling over with enthusiasm, couldn't wait to get out every morning, to run races with Barbie, or play croquet, or above all, to hunt down crickets. He had been reading Chinese poetry and history and wanted to see if he could manage to catch crickets of different tones and so have a private cricket orchestra. This was just the sort of thing Barbie loved and pretty soon they went off together on picnics, the pretext to find crickets far afield, crickets of another valley whose voices might by a happy chance be a half-tone shriller than those of the demesne. At last Barbie had a friend! The whole family sighed with relief, and there was much speculating among the parents. They would all have been pleased at the match, though of course the children were both far too young at present—eighteen exactly. Philip's birthday was to take place while he was with them. The Olivers were

58

persuaded to stay on another week to celebrate it with a dance.

Violet saw as if it were yesterday the clouded look that came over Barbie's face. "Why a dance?" she said brusquely. "Dances bore Philip—and after all it's his birthday."

Violet saw Philip's bright glancing eyes and his amused response. "Why not a dance? I think it's a charming idea, Mrs. Dene," and he waltzed solemnly alone across the hall holding an imaginary partner in his arms. Barbie got up and left the room.

Did he then have any idea of the intensity of Barbie's feelings, so that this dismissal of her plea seemed like a betrayal, the first crack in a solidarity she had taken for granted?

When Violet made an excuse to go out and find her sister, Barbie was cold with anger, sitting on the bench on the landing looking out into the night. "Go away," she said. "You don't understand."

"It'll be fun, Barbie, you can wear your new red dress. You'll look like a flame dancing . . ." and then as there was no response Violet added, "Besides you and Philip can escape into the garden. No one will notice."

But Barbie had withdrawn into a citadel of unhappiness and would not come out. Philip himself was bewildered by the change in her, and did nothing to make things better by playing croquet with Violet the next morning, since Barbie was nowhere to be found.

Then they were all caught up in the preparations.

The silence was broken by an irruption of waltzes and polkas, which Mrs. Dene would break off suddenly as she remembered something she should still do. There would be claret cup, not champagne after all—it was really too expensive. The Olivers and the Denes made innumerable secret trips into town in the Olivers' Bentley, coming back exhausted, laden with packages and dramatic stories of flat tires. There were endless talks between the women about what each should wear. Barbie meanwhile took refuge in the kitchen—her contribution was to go out alone and gather mushrooms for Annie.

On the night of the dance itself Violet and her mother walked one last time through the rooms, giving a final touch to the flowers, sliding tentatively on the freshly waxed floors from which all the rugs had been taken up. It was a perfect July evening, the outer green dark reflected in the long mirrors, with points of candle flame like lights coming up through water flaring through them, and roses transformed into subaqueous flowers. Violet remembered her tremor of intoxicating stage fright like an actress surveying the stage where she would make her entrance—it looked so empty now, the grand piano pulled off into the far end where the orchestra (two violins, a 'cello and the piano player) would sit. And then she had run out to find Barbie, to help Barbie dress and to be sure she did her hair properly. Wouldn't Barbie, couldn't she just this once, because of Philip, rise to the occasion? If she could have a great success, how wonderful it would be! Then Violet could feel wholly free to be her own most charming and adorable self, could drink in the admiring glances without a shadow of guilt, could choose from all the faces the one she would make hers for the evening.

What could she have done that she didn't do if she had guessed whose this face would be tonight? Was it her fault, when Barbie vanished after the first five dances, that Philip came to her, his eyes shining, stammering with excitement.

"I s-say. It's my birthday, you know. Do you think I might have one dance?"

He looked quite different in his evening clothes, taller, though not quite tall enough to look down at Violet. Their eyes met on the level, a single startled look of recognition which neither of them risked again during that dance.

"Where's Barbie?" Violet asked as if nothing had happened, when he let her go after the waltz and they stood for a moment in the window, breathing in the delicious warm night air. "Hadn't you better try to find her? Bring her back?"

Philip looked embarrassed. "She's in some queer mood," he said, "I don't think she wants to be followed about."

"Didn't she look lovely, though? Why does she hate dances?" Violet asked, longing for help, longing for Philip to break off, release her from the queer insistent weight she felt around her heart.

"Come out"—Philip's cheeks burned with his daring—"let's look for her together!"

"Oh no, that would never do." Violet was mercifully interrupted to dance the next waltz with her father.

"What a nice boy he is," her father said. "I was hoping Barbie would emerge from her cocoon tonight, but she seems to have vanished," and Mr. Dene sighed. There were twenty invited guests but Violet felt as if the Denes were dancing alone, as if no one else existed on this night when everything, her mother's unusually brilliant look, seemed lifted up to a pitch of unreal intensity. "I wish we could help Barbie . . ." she could hear her father's gentle voice, troubled, over the sweet insistent violins that cried, "Dance, dance, don't think—just feel—"

Finally she was twirling, twirling alone with Philip, the red rose she had pinned to her pale blue dress breaking apart so a petal fell here and another there and still they danced until the sound of repeated "good nights" in the hall woke Violet from her trance and she saw Barbie standing in the doorway.

"Darling," she ran across the floor as if she could run away from all that had happened, "where have you been?"

"Out," Barbie said shortly. And then without looking at Violet she turned to Philip with a queer pleading look and said, "I think I've found a cricket for you with a new note."

How could Barbie know that Philip had suffered a metamorphosis and that hereafter a cricket with a new note would mean next to nothing to him? Barbie too had grown up over night. Without any of the preliminaries, the flirtations, the withdrawals, the experiments which were usual in girls of her age, she had just exploded in one brilliant shower of fire and tears, had moved over into womanhood. She was deeply and entirely in love at the precise instant when Philip was turning his back on her, thinking of her as part of a child world which he had suddenly outgrown. From the night of the ball on through almost two years Barbie and Violet entered a tunnel of strain and misery. It was as if the dance had been a final carefree time, never to happen again. The unusual brilliance of their mother that evening had been partly due to a fever and she had to spend the next year in Switzerland. Their father, harassed by unforeseen expenses, going over to see his wife every month, seemed hardly to know what was happening, and Miss Goddard, who came back to chaperone if not teach her former charges, still treated Barbie as if she were a child.

"I couldn't undo what I'd done," Violet said bitterly, "though I asked Philip almost at once to stop writing to me." It had not even been a great sacrifice (which might have made Violet feel less guilty) for she had not of course been in love with Philip. It had just been an evening of delight and recognition; he had not even kissed her. For Barbie it had been a tragedy, a tragedy which she cherished, which she refused to accept and be sensible about, and which focused in a brilliant hard light all her repressed resentment of her older sister.

Violet began by being sympathetic but ended by being impatient and scornful. The rift between them in a year had become so wide that they had never since been able to cross it.

"I should have thought that all that would have seemed pretty childish to Barbie herself by the time she married," Charles said. The moonlight was still there, just as calm and bright as before, all around them, but even Charles was aware that to Violet this rather simple story had some symbolic significance far out of proportion with its actual facts. She was actually trembling.

"Oh by then the harm was done. By then we had become enemies." And she added, "By then I had come to hate myself, which was far worse."

"I don't understand . . ." Charles said kindly, but he could not quite conceal a yawn.

"Poor darling, you've been as patient as Job. Go to sleep."

"What about closing the shutters? We'll never go to sleep in this moonlight." And Charles, eager to do something, got up and padded barefoot across the cold floor. A powerful scent of earth and grass came up to him from the garden below. This all seemed so sane beside the intense and, to him, exaggerated feelings of his wife in the bed behind him that he was glad to look out, and indeed suddenly didn't want to close the shutters, to close them in.

"Don't," came the voice from the bed. "It's so lovely . . ." so he left them open, fumbling on the

64

dresser for a cigarette, and bringing one and an ashtray to Violet.

"So Barbie never wanted to come back once she had left—it was the place of intensest feeling."

"And yet you did want to come back," Charles said. Violet's point of view about things never failed to interest him, even when it seemed quite mad.

"Oh, I was afraid, of course—I haven't gone into Barbie's room yet, you know. But the house is so much more than all that, that one episode, devastating as it was. There are times here when one's personal feelings seem irrelevant."

"I wonder what Sally will think . . ." The question lay on the moonlit air, and had its own reverberations in Violet's mind through the night. A great deal would depend of course on whether the life she and Charles were precariously creating here was powerful enough to combat an idée fixe. It would in any case, she foresaw, be a battle, and she could not deny that she dreaded it.

The day finally came, the day about which there had
been so much speculation, argument, and excitement,
the day when Charles was to go off to Shannon and
fetch Sally. It was a soft brilliant morning, Charles had
been glad to see. And now as he ate his breakfast the
sun lit up the wall of portraits just across the table from
him. Some were so dim, that of Colonel Dene, the
Cromwell Dene, especially, that it took this morning
light to make his features visible. Charles amused himself this morning by marshalling them one by one, by
name, and wondering which of all these, if any would
be repeated in the youngest Dene he was about to bring
home. Would Sally have a fanatic streak like old Colonel Dene and Sarah St. Leger—the enthusiasts? Would
she be practical and managing like her great grandfather Jonas Oliver? Or turn into a selfish, intelligent
eccentric old maid like Tomasine who liked horses so
much better than people and had been painted in riding
habit with a hunting dog at her feet? Or would she be
rather dim and sweet and keep herself a secret like one

66

or two of the women staring out smugly, telling nothing of themselves? Charles felt quite pleasantly excited at the idea of an unknown Dene coming toward them now out of the future (in a plane at 600 miles an hour) instead of out of the past, as all these others had loomed up and taken on definite character in his mind.

It was a relief too that the suspense would soon be over. And as Charles ran up the stairs two at a time (though he was annoyed to find that he was quite breathless at the first landing), he felt that after all it was a very good thing indeed that their first weeks of settling in should have this climax.

Hours later Violet looked up at the house behind her, unsoftened by the evening light, then turned her back to it, and a solitary figure on the terrace, peered short-sightedly down the drive, at the familiar curve of the hill before her, at the grove of oaks, very dark now as the late afternoon sun made the grass shine all around them. This distant view was healing as if the landscape softened and distilled anxiety as it softened and sheltered the great house, standing aloof in its hollow. She stood there for some time, smoking a cigarette, more nervous than she admitted to herself, before she heard the gate clang at last and the purr of the car. Then she ran back a moment into the house to look at herself in the glass door, peering anxiously at her face which some trick of reflection turned all crooked, knotted the pale blue chiffon scarf more firmly under her chin, and walked back onto the terrace like an actress making an entrance, smiling into the air, lifting her chin slightly —and knowing she was being absurd.

"Well, here we are!"

Violet knew at once by Charles's busyness, his efficiency, that they must have stopped several times on the way. A small dark head had stooped to pick up her handbag which had dropped on the bottom step. Now two dark eyes looked straight up into Violet's eyes.

"Are we here? I don't know where I am, but you must be Aunt Violet. Hi, Aunt Violet," said the girl and promptly fell down, instead, as she no doubt meant to, of running up the steps.

"Good gracious, child, did you hurt yourself?" Violet took in the bright eyes, the flushed face.

"I don't know, but I can't possibly get up. Everything's going round and round." She was laughing helplessly, apparently unaware that her knee was bleeding through the torn stocking. And this casual incompetence was so entirely like Barbie that Violet felt the old exasperated tenderness mounting; I would really like to shake her, Violet thought. It was a bit much to arrive drunk.

"Silly little fool, give me your hand," Charles was saying firmly. And then to Violet, "Tell Annie to make some strong coffee and get a bandage for heaven's sake. Don't just stand there looking like an angel of mercy and doing nothing."

By the time Violet came back with the bandage, Sally was installed on the big sofa in the library, softened in some way by the firelight, by the great bunch of zinnias and roses behind her, so small and helpless-looking in the vast proportions of the room that she gave the impression of a bright-eyed, frightened fledgeling.

"I'm terribly sorry," she said while Violet stooped down to bandage the knee with deft quick fingers. "But I feel so strange, such a rough flight and—well . . ." She did not finish, for how could she say what she felt, which was that when she had looked up at the high bleak stone face of the house, it had seemed a prison? It had frightened her. She was ignorance itself, had never seen a picture of the house, thought of Ireland as little white thatched cottages, donkey carts.

"There," Violet said, giving the knee a gentle pat, "by tomorrow you'll be all right."

"Fit as a fiddle," Charles added for good measure.

But what would she do when she felt fit, Sally asked herself with something like despair? Whatever would she do here? It might as well have been the moon, so far, so cut off from everything familiar did she feel. And this was what caused her dizziness, not the two small whiskeys she had had with Charles on the way (he seemed like a hero in a British film, so clipped and sure of himself, and, she suspected, finding her funny for reasons she could not know). When she had fallen she had still felt in command, a person in her own right, but ever since it was as if her power to be herself were leaking away, as if she were diminished, smaller than when she arrived. Was it only this very high room which made even Charles look insignificant standing by the fire, pushing the tobacco down in his pipe, saying to Violet, "We'll take her for a drive tomorrow"?

She was afraid she would begin to cry when a maid, blushing profusely, came in with the coffee. They called her Maire. She looked about fifteen, was terribly shy, shyer even than Sally herself felt. She had very red hands and was clumsy about arranging things. This endeared her at once to Sally, who no longer felt like crying.

The coffee was unbelievably weak and watery, but it was hot and she drank two cups, and then took out a cigarette. It was time to make an effort at politeness.

"Mother has told me so much about the house, but I couldn't imagine it." She looked up at the long windows through which the late afternoon light was streaming, and she felt the silence, inside this high room filled with books, and outside where there was nothing to see but trees and meadows and hills. "I should think it would be lonely in winter," she added.

"We only came here in the holidays, you know,"

Violet said half-apologetically, "we never really lived here."

"It's so funny to think of mother here," Sally said. "What was she like?" For the first time she dared to look at her aunt. She did not look like a famous beauty at all. She looked rather tired and sad, and much older than Sally's mother, as well as different in every way, so Sally thought, waiting for some gesture, some look to which she could attach herself, which would mean, Yes, this is my family, this is my blood.

"What was Barbie like?" Violet asked herself, stretching out her thin heavily ringed hands to the fire. "Not a bit like you," she said. "No, not a bit like you," she repeated and laughed a laugh so musical and clear that in its sound Sally read what it was to have been a beauty, the slightly staged charm of the laugh. "Your mother was the most absent-minded, dreamy, careless maddening little girl whose shoelaces were always coming undone, who had a passion for climbing trees, and who was never to be found when wanted."

"Was she?" Sally opened her eyes wide. "I never could imagine," for her mother seemed solidity and safety itself, sitting at a little desk by the window, writing letters, always with a list in her pocketbook, organizing everything. "But that's rather like me." She understood suddenly why Aunt Violet had laughed, and blushed.

"Well," Charles interrupted, "if we've finished our coffee, I suggest that Sally be helped upstairs on her

uncle's arm and have a chance to wash and unpack."
He looked at his watch. "It's seven. Dinner's at eight.
We might have a cocktail at a quarter to, so you haven't
much time."

"Don't bother to change," Violet said quickly. After
all, Sally hardly needed the kindly arms, as they pro-
ceeded up the wide staircase three abreast, across the
landing, and then through a door into a dark narrow
corridor where Violet went ahead, leading the way up
a steep staircase, up and up and finally out into a low-
ceilinged enormous room which Sally was told, had
been the ballroom. They crossed it to a far door at the
right, her door.

"You'll find hot water in the jug," Aunt Violet was
saying. The suitcases were already open on their stands.
Then suddenly Sally was alone.

She looked around the room with the wary look of a
prisoner as the door clicks behind him in his cell. The
jug in the washstand was swathed in towels. Perhaps,
Sally thought, if I washed—but it seemed almost insu-
perably difficult to find what she needed in the open
suitcases. She fumbled about, flinging shoes to the floor,
taking out nightgowns and underwear and throwing
them on the bed, so that within a few minutes the disorder was frightening and she felt overcome with impotence and fatigue. At this moment, without having
washed, she lay down on the bed crosswise on top of
the chaos of garments, and closed her eyes. Then pain-
fully, as she had fumbled among her real belongings,
she began to try to find her way back across all the hours

of flight to something she was carrying with her, which seemed her one real possession, and this was her feeling for Ian. As long as she could find this and hang on to it, whatever happened, she knew that she could remain herself. For what had been frightening was the sense, ever since she had fallen on the terrace steps, that herself was slowly being dispersed or flowing away. Ian, she murmured half aloud. But the queer thing was that she couldn't focus on him; she couldn't see him. She realized with panic that his image was blurred.

This roused her at once. She got up, found the silver frame in the bottom of her small blue bag, and set it down beside the bowl of roses. Now she had his face again, the theatrical smile, the very black hair and fine cheekbones, the languorous laughing eyes. (Oh how beautiful he is, she thought, the sensation of her love sharply there like a stab just under her heart—and it was this sensation she needed to feel herself, as a drug addict must have his piqûre.) Now she became efficient. She lifted the heavy jug, poured out water in the basin and washed. Then she put on a clean white blouse and her little red jacket. Finally she went to the mirror, powdered, and drew a line of lipstick firmly across her mouth.

Quite unconsciously she had ignored the room. She had not examined it. She had not even looked out of the windows. In no way must she yield to these surroundings if she was to keep hold of her real self. If the idea was that a summer in Ireland would make her forget, they would find out. When she looked around the mess she had made, she felt queerly satisfied. It was her first victory.

But when she found herself outside her own door, she realized again the extraordinary palpitating silence, and hesitated to break it by venturing out onto the great open spaces of the ballroom floor as if a footstep might crash instead of creaking. Finally she tiptoed across to the safety of the back stairs.

This was the time of day Violet liked best. She wore black velvet, a high choker of pearls, and had a moment always of narcissistic pleasure when she was putting perfume behind her ears, for the high candles on the dressing table softened the lines, and just before dinner each evening she knew again that she had been beautiful. She heard Sally stumble on the landing and went out to meet her.

"How is your knee, Sally? Does it hurt?" she asked solicitously, putting a tentative hand on the stiff rather soldierly shoulder in its red jacket.

"I haven't thought"—Sally turned, frowning. "It does hurt, I guess," she added vaguely. She had not stumbled because her knee hurt, but because emerging into this wide landing had startled her after the dark staircase.

"You must stay in bed tomorrow morning and have a long good rest. Only Charles goes down for breakfast."

"Oh, I always get up," Sally said definitely, the rebuff intentional. With this they arrived at the library through the back door.

"Darling, how lovely to have a drink!" Violet curled up in the armchair, looking up at her husband with a radiant smile. Sally observed this. She did not want to be loved by these people, nor to love them, but the knowledge that she must not made her feel queerly sad.

"Well, funny little face"—Charles turned from the table in the corner where he was mixing drinks—"What are you allowed to have? A martini?"

"Yes, please, Uncle Charles."

In spite of herself, Sally was aware that her Aunt Violet looked rather beautiful, in a disturbing slightly elderly way which suggested a knowledge of life and a security which she envied. Would Ian think she was beautiful, she wondered? Or would he say, as she had heard him once about a fashionable woman who sent him an orchid, "That old bag!"

"A penny for your thoughts," Charles said teasingly as he handed her a glass.

"Ian," she said simply. "It's always Ian when someone want to know my thoughts."

Charles and Violet exchanged a look. Should they

75

ignore this or press it further? It was Violet who said quietly,

"Your Ian must be a great charmer."

"Women fall for him, of course," Sally said with possessive contempt. "In a way, it's part of his job."

"Yes, I see," said Violet. "That must be rather a bore for you sometimes."

"Oh no." The candor was disarming. "They're his trophies, like silver cups if he were an athlete. He brings them all to me."

"But after all," Charles was unaware that what he felt was jealousy, "this fellow's nothing but an actor, what? You're not serious, Sally?"

"Charles—" Violet warned, but it was too late.

"You sound like my mother, Uncle Charles," Sally was carefully condescending. She drank her martini down at one gulp. She was dead sober now, watchful as a mother cat protecting her kittens. She was going to win the first round, she must. "I suppose"—she turned now to her aunt—"that Mother told you we are engaged."

"Yes," Violet lied, "I think she said something of the sort." Actually what Barbie had written was that Sally would tell them she was engaged, but that Ian had no intention of marrying her and had told Barbie so himself. For a second Violet wondered if her sister were telling the truth. "But you'll finish college before you get married, surely?"

"I suppose so. That's the bargain I've made with Mother. Daddy has washed his hands of the whole

76

business, thank God," Sally said and laughed a short, not very happy laugh. "By the way, I don't suppose there were any letters for me?"

"You've only been gone twenty-four hours, you know," Charles teased.

"It seems like a year." With this, said very quietly, Sally looked once around the room, at the great shelves of books mounting to the ceiling, at the closed cabinet along one side with its fine bindings, at the long windows and the firelight flaming through them. She shivered.

Violet saw the shiver. "You must be very tired." Sally felt the net of tenderness falling down over her like a spell. From the moment she had fallen down on the front steps, she had known there was a spell here, and she would have to fight like mad not to be caught in it.

"Mostly," she said with something like violence, "I'm mad."

Charles chuckled. Violet informed him that in America "mad" means "angry." Then he chuckled even more.

"A little angry thing has come to stay," he said happily. "A little mad thing too, perhaps?"

But Sally said nothing. She would not look at them. She would remain intact.

"Does the little mad thing play golf?" he persisted. It seemed, as they went in to dinner, that she did. But Sally felt so diminished sitting beneath the high wall entirely filled with family portraits, that she ate the whole meal in silence. Charles and Violet, having by tacit agreement given up trying to draw her out, flirted across the long table. Sally observed this. It was quite unlike the behavior of her own parents who took each other for granted. She found that she was becoming curious, perhaps even slightly entranced by this marriage she was to contemplate for two months, by this pair between whom she sat, not quite a stranger.

The next morning she did not, after all, play golf. Her knee was rather stiff. Instead she got Radio-Luxembourg on the powerful portable radio she had brought with her, and played jazz all morning. Downstairs Violet thought the house rejected this so violently that the very walls sent it back, echoing. She fled into the walled garden and weeded with passion, but even there strange wails and barbaric yawps reached her. The occupation, she thought with a grim smile, has begun.

When Maire came finally to do the room, Sally went down to the library and sat at the huge desk where her grandfather had studied his briefs. There she composed a careful letter to Ian. It was so careful that she copied it out twice.

O Ian, I am so far away and it is all so queer here. This morning I got *La Vie en Rose* from somewhere in Europe. This made it all seem stranger for a while, and now I am sitting at a very big desk in the library thinking about us. I have to keep thinking about us or I would die here, in this prison. My Uncle Charles teases me and does not understand anything, which is a great relief. He is still terribly in love with Aunt Violet. I wonder if you would think her lovely. She is trying to get at me, but I shan't let her. You see, it's the only way I can keep us safe from harm, from all harm, my darling, until we meet again. The worst of all is your kisses. Sally.

Her feeling was so intense that Sally could never write otherwise to Ian. She was reduced to what she considered an idiotic simplicity where he was concerned. Anything else seemed like lies and literature, the sort of letter she used to write to her English teacher at school, full of quotations from Keats and Shelley. The level on which she communicated with Ian was so different from any spoken language that she sometimes felt it useless to write and hardly read his letters except to see how he signed. They were always about himself, but sometimes they began "Darling," and sometimes they did not end with just "love, Ian," but dear things like "Keep hoping, love" or "You're my best girl."

She had forgotten where she was when Uncle Charles came in from behind and put two earth-smelling hands over her eyes.

"Oh," she said, then quickly, not to yield to him even her surprise, "Of course, it's you, Uncle Charles."

"Not of course. It might be a strange young man fresh from Oxford." Charles was feeling cheerful. The foreign occupation was putting them on their mettle. Even Cammaert had grumbled about the roses with new interest.

"A few days like this," he said, squinting up at the luminous haze which suggested the presence of sunlight somewhere, if not precisely here, "and we might get some late bloom. Damn damp country," he added as if he had gone too far.

Sally did not comment on her uncle's fantasy about a young man who did not interest her even as a figure of the imagination.

"I shall have to get some stamps, Uncle Charles."

"Leave it on the hall table," he said casually. "The postman will see to that," he said, as if, Sally thought, they had a special privilege of free stamps. Did the postman keep an account? But Uncle Charles interrupted her revery, the letter in her hand, "Come out and take a look at the day!"

"When does the postman come?" she asked. She would have liked to stand guard over her letter herself and lay it carefully in the postman's hand. But she was afraid of Charles's teasing, so she followed him slowly into the hall and laid the frail little envelope carefully on top of a small pile in Violet's pronounced hand.

Charles noticed her backward glance as he held the glass door open for her to go through. This Victorian addition bothered his sense of style. Charles did not as yet love the house, but he respected it, as he respected good boots and well-cut old clothes. Sloppiness, lack of form bothered him. Sally's blue jeans, too tight he thought, with an absurd boy's checked shirt with the tails out over them, bothered him very much.

"You do look rather queer," he said not unkindly. "Is that the usual thing?"

"Yes." As a matter of fact, she had felt uncouth, standing by the great bed reflected in the oval mirror in the dressing table in her room. But she had put on these things deliberately. She was going to remain wholly and defiantly American.

They stood for a moment on the terrace while Charles lit his pipe, and asked with it between his teeth, "Do you think your knee would bear a walk up the hill? From there you really see the house, how it lies in the hollow."

Sally stood there, her hands in her pockets, androgynous, remote as a sulky schoolboy. During the night she seemed to have changed or else he had first seen her in the rosy light of arrival, of drinks, and the solicitude caused by her fall. He did not, at the moment, find her attractive.

They plodded up the hill on the uneven ground where the frost had made bumps and the coarse grass crunched under their feet, and did not talk. It was high time O'Neil brought the sheep over, Charles was thinking. Sally, whose knee hurt rather a lot, was absorbed in the effort of the walk. She did not, he noticed, look back once at the house. Charles turned this indifference of hers over in his mind. The vagaries of women interested him. He imagined that he knew a good deal about them. Violet, who found this convenient, had never disabused him of the idea. Still, it was strange that Sally showed so little curiosity. After all, her grandfather had lived here. Her mother had spent her first seventeen summers here. He was puzzled.

They had now almost reached the rather straggly forest that circled the top of the bowl.

"There—" he laid his hands on Sally's passive shoulders and forced them to turn round—"there's Dene's Court."

To Sally it looked as ugly and unyielding as the prison she had found it at first glance. It was so complete in itself, planted flat against the trees, that even the beds of flowers and lawn to the right did nothing to soften it, and themselves looked only slightly out of proportion. She stared at it, fascinated in spite of herself, as if she and it were pivoted against each other. She could not have said that it was not alive. It was very much alive. For just a second she had one of those moments of illumination when time falls away, felt she was already nothing, melted into air, that in fact it had already won. To dissipate this vision which she could not accept, she took out a cigarette and tried to think of something rude but true to say. What she achieved was rather petty, after all.

"I don't like it, Uncle Charles." She frowned at the house as if she were trying to communicate her frown to its stone face, to evoke some response, so intently did she watch the open windows.

"Why not?" Charles asked. "There aren't so many of these houses left you know." He watched her, still frowning at it. "It's rather a rarity. Most of them were burned in what the Irish call The Troubles." He wondered if she had heard, and repeated his question, "Why don't you like it, Sally?"

"It's—" she searched for a word—"awkward," she said, turning to him with the kind of defiance he supposed she called "mad." "It's uncomfortable. It looks like a stranger here."

She looked away from the stone face with relief, looked at the repose of the hills, the reconciliation of the trees with the hills behind it. And so she was not watching when Violet, who had caught sight of them from her window on the second floor, leaned out and waved.

"There's Violet!"

Sally, instead of waving, turned to watch Charles wave, feeling again the connection between these two magnetic poles; she was moved now by the smallness of the fair head in the window, leaning out, by its frailty against all that stone, and by the pleasure Charles clearly took in this moment of childish communication.

"My mother, I suppose, minded Violet being so beautiful," she said when Violet had disappeared, leaving the window strangely empty and lonely without her.

"I suppose so." Charles was not going to yield up his wife's secrets to this queer little niece.

"But she married before Aunt Violet did?"

"Yes, some time before, so actually, I never knew your mother . . ."

That was all Charles had to say, Sally felt, so she turned down the hill again, this time towards the left to come out on the drive and spare her knee the uneven descent through the humpy grassbed.

When they reached the drive, Charles said in a low voice as if he was very conscious of Violet somewhere near-by, "I wouldn't say much about the house to Violet, Sally. She might be hurt. You see, the house means a great deal to her, and after all," he added, "we have to live here. We have to make the best of it."

To this plea Sally made no reply. She was not going to be part of any pact with anyone here. But she made a note of it, as a weapon she might one day wish to use.

That night, safe at last in the great bed on the second floor, Violet and Charles lay side by side in the dark. "For instance," Violet was saying, "I thought it a bit much to come down to dinner in those slacks."

"At least," Charles chuckled, "she had tucked in her shirttails."

"Her room looks like a pigpen. She has moved the furniture about so it has no shape or reason. She hadn't even hung up her dresses when I went up there this afternoon. She's a perfect savage!" They lay on their backs talking up into the dark, enjoying themselves.

"She's in love, Violet," Charles said in his smug all-understanding tone of voice.

"Rubbish. When I was in love I didn't throw my clothes all over the place and refuse to dress for dinner."

"Well, you weren't shipped off across an ocean to forget me. I was considered rather eligible, I believe." Charles was enjoying himself. He loved to get Violet angry, to feel the electricity in her small impatient hand which withdrew itself violently three times as he tried to clasp it.

"No, Charles, please, I won't be pacified," she said in a cross caressing voice. "It's going to be a horrible summer and all I want is peace."

"You don't want peace at all. You never have wanted peace," Charles answered in his omniscient tone. "What you want is to be loved and adored, and as this hasn't yet happened in Sally's case, you are disgruntled."

"Does she love and adore you then?" Violet was on the defensive, for what he had said was unfortunately true. It was true, she did need love, praise, the aura in which she had moved since she was a small child. When she did not feel the aura, which had to be created by other people, she was miserable, diminished. She hated herself.

"Well"—Violet was unable to see his wicked smile in the dark—"I'm a man. She's a susceptible young girl—"

"Charles!" Violet sat straight up and tried to see his face. Then as she heard him chuckle, she beat his hard chest with her two fists, "You monster!" They were enjoying themselves enormously.

"She doesn't like either of us, and she hates the house, and that, if you want it, is the truth," Charles said finally for he was getting sleepy. He had been out with Cammaert all afternoon.

"Oh." Violet lay down again and thought this over. When she asked him how he knew Sally hated the house, she heard a gentle grunt and realized that he was fast asleep.

She lay wide awake in the dark and looked up at the ceiling as if she could somehow feel her way through into the room above. How often she had lain awake like this worrying over her sister, Barbie, blaming herself for arousing a jealousy she could do nothing to assuage. Was Sally asleep she wondered? Lonely? Perhaps weeping those fierce tears one weeps at twenty and never again, because never again is love so pure, so impossible? Women, she thought, are helpless, having to accept the decisions of other people, so rarely able to act directly and for themselves. More than sons ever do, they take care of and arrange their lives round the lives of parents, and then around the lives of husbands and children. In Sally there was still the implacable wish to become herself all by herself. So she would suffer, perhaps a great deal, before she learned to accept life as it is. But why must we accept it, Violet asked the dark? Is it that in accepting it we finally accept ourselves? But I, she thought, have never accepted myself—perhaps because I have never been loved for myself as an ugly woman may be. I have only been loved for something over which I have no control and did not make. The proof is, she thought bitterly, that now this beauty is going, I am no longer loved in the same way. Even Charles feels the difference. He loves me because of his memory of what I was. But he does not see me as I am now, and he will never guess how terribly afraid I am that he someday will. We have never been friends, she thought, curling herself now against the unconscious warmth beside her, we have only been lovers. So it seemed that their whole life together had been a game played over an abyss—and only she saw the abyss, or was beginning to see it. Charles was still intent upon the game. The impact of the presence of a young girl had made this terribly clear to her, all of it. And Violet was suddenly afraid of what the summer would show.

In the next few days, Sally, enclosed in her cocoon of determined indifference, did not find life easy. She was never quite comfortable. Every morning she shut herself up after breakfast and got every station in Europe which could provide jazz. But this was a painful kind of pleasure because she felt without perhaps quite admitting it, that the house, the room rejected the radio. She was doing something by force which could only be fun if it belonged. Jazz was the climate of her relationship with Ian, who for some reason loved to talk about very serious things like Strindberg against a loud background of jazz in some small very crowded Harlem night club. There was no way to transplant this climate, and trying only made her feel farther away and desperate. She was always outside everything now, never inside anything, except just before she went to sleep when she re-enacted every meeting with Ian and often dreamed sensuous dreams which made her wake up feeling slightly ashamed and very tired.

She was obscurely aware that any regular rhythm of life creates a spell and ends by taming one. But everything about this house and her aunt and uncle was built on rhythm and ritual, even something as apparently casual as her walk up the hill on the first morning. Things like tea in the afternoon, dressing for dinner, the moment on the terrace before lunch, Aunt Violet arranging the great massive bouquets of flowers in the library, were all part of the spell Sally must keep breaking or be caught. So whenever she could she interrupted or broke arranged plans. She went out for a walk and did not come back for tea, or missed the cocktail hour altogether and came down to dinner in slacks.

She had quite deliberately avoided establishing anything like a relationship with Annie to whom Violet had of course taken her to make a solemn presentation. Sally reacted to this rather like a small hedgehog who curls up into a tight ball and presents only prickles towards an outstretched hand. She said something about being glad to meet Annie, and then stood, eyes cast down, only waiting to be allowed to escape. She had felt at once that if she did not want to be drawn into the life here, Annie was her most formidable antagonist. Just the way Annie had taken her for granted, smiled at her not as at a stranger but as an old friend, turning to Violet to say with astonished pleasure, "She's the image of her Grannie, Miss Violet—why didn't you tell me?"

Violet laughed, "Dear Annie, to me Grannie always seemed so very old." They had looked at Sally as if she were an object and Violet added, "I see what you mean, the eyes—yes . . ."

"The dear stubborn look of her," said Annie as if Sally's deliberate ill manners were only an added proof of virtue. "When you're settled and have time, I shall have to be hearing all about your mother," Annie said as they made to go. But from then on Sally avoided the kitchen, though she was never unaware of the magnet below, the magnet of Annie and all she could tell Sally about her mother, the warmth and simplicity of Annie which seemed so restful after Violet's subtleties—yet she would not go. She must resist, even when Maire in the mornings dropped hints that Annie would like to see her, that Annie was hurt.

"I can't do it, Maire," Sally had said shortly. "I can't be caught."

With Maire alone she had a relationship. Perhaps they recognized in each other a capacity for obsession, perhaps in this house where they alone were young they made an unconscious pact. Maire had not answered this last. The best thing about Maire was that she never talked. What Annie heard about Sally she heard from Violet. When Violet grew impatient and complained of

Sally's unco-operating attitude, Annie just poured her another cup of tea and nodded her head,

"Bide your time," she said. "She'll come round. No Dene could live in this house a month and not get caught—whatever she may say, whatever she may do," Annie said. "Besides, she'll begin to love you, Miss Violet, she'll not be able to resist you."

It was quite true that in spite of all the walls she threw up, Sally was immensely curious about the relationship between her aunt and uncle. When she came into a room where they were sitting, Charles with a book perhaps, Violet doing her interminable petit point, she had the feeling of interrupting a conversation, though they had been sitting in complete silence. They looked up at her then as if they had been startled out of a moment of physical intimacy, were even a little embarrassed, and Charles spoke rather loudly, with emphasis, as if he had been talking before in a secret voice which he feared might have been overheard.

Sally found that she wanted to know where they were and what they were doing and if she didn't know she felt lost. It amused her to have the power to interrupt the rituals. She went down deliberately one morning for this purpose, and found her aunt as she knew she would find her, before a jumble of roses and lupin and foxglove lying loosely on newspapers spread over the big table in the library. She stood for a moment and watched her aunt look from the flowers to the Chinese Lowestoft bowl and back again in absent-minded concentration. Then Sally sat down on the arm of one of the worn brown velvet armchairs, swinging her sore knee for practise.

"It's going to rain again," Aunt Violet announced to no one in particular or perhaps to the foxglove she held in her hand, measuring it against space as if she were a painter. "A little shorter, I think," she murmured. This business of arranging the flowers was a meditation. She hated to be interrupted in the middle, or to be watched. There was always the moment when the whole thing refused to make a whole, when for ten minutes or more she took out, cut down, shifted one flower or another—and in fact was never satisfied. She shook the dew out of a fat pink moss rose and looked thoughtfully at its face, then smelled it—or rather, Sally thought watching her, drank it.

At this moment clouds must have swept over the sun for the room was suddenly dark, so dark that it was hard to see. Sally had never been in a house where the outside weather was so important, and as the outside weather never remained the same for more than a few hours, this too added to her feeling of suspense, of un-reality. Now heavy straight rain poured down.

"Oh dear, the roses!" Violet said with an air of such desolation that Sally felt forced to ask, "What about the roses? They're all right, it seems to me."

"Not these, but the bed in the walled garden. They will all fall in the rain."

Sally laughed, "Sometimes, Aunt Violet, you sound like a ham actor."

"Do I? Whatever do you mean?" Violet took out the

Canterbury bell she had just carefully placed, and put it back again, just a little more towards the center.

"Oh, I don't know," Sally swung her leg. It wasn't worth explaining something rude to someone who was wholly absorbed in something else.

But Violet was nettled, was being deliberately obtuse, and now had her revenge, "Have you heard from Ian?" she asked.

"No." Sally blushed to the roots of her hair with misery. For now it had been nearly a week and she had not heard. "I expect he's got a summer theatre job and is much too busy learning lines. I'm not worried," she said giving herself away by the very emphasis with which she said it.

"Perhaps there'll be a letter this morning," Violet said, ashamed of herself for yielding to such a petty impulse to hurt. "Yes, surely there'll be a letter, you'll see." She stood back to get the effect of the flowers, then swiftly took out two foxgloves. At this moment the whole bunch flopped over sideways. She was wildly irritated with Sally, impervious, self-absorbed, waiting for a letter and meanwhile discomposing, so it seemed, the whole world around her.

"Damn," said Violet.

"Are you saying that to me or the flowers?" Sally asked mischievously.

"Both. I can't do this and talk," Violet was crosser than seemed rational but she couldn't help it.

"Then give up the flowers and talk to me." Sally fell down comfortably into the chair, her legs swung over

93

the arm. She felt that she was dominating the moment, that it was she for once and not the implacable ritual which had won.

"But I can't leave the room in this mess!" Violet stooped to pick up the newspapers and was astonished to see a quick brown hand ahead of her. Sally was actually helping. "Oh, that's a dear child," she said and stood up with relief. Stooping made her feel a bit dizzy.

"Now," Sally commanded when she had righted the flowers, stuck the two foxgloves back carelessly, and rolled the newspapers up, "let me make you a very mild gin and lime, Aunt Violet, and sit down and talk to me." This sense of power was intoxicating. "Why can't you leave a room in a mess for half an hour?" Sally asked, handing her aunt a glass.

Violet was standing by the fireplace, amused, pleased in spite of herself at so much attention from the implacable Sally. "I don't know," she said thoughtfully, "I suppose it makes me feel uncomfortable. I couldn't live in a room like yours," she parried.

"I don't live there," Sally said, frowning.

"Where do you live then?" Violet watched the darkening face and thought Sally looked like a fury at times, a self-contained little fury who might begin murdering or destroying things at any moment. The rain stopped as suddenly as it began, and the silence made Sally's words sound louder than she had intended.

"I don't know." The question opened up a great emptiness around and within her. For did she live at home

94

where her family disapproved of Ian so constantly and evidently? At college which was only another prison? With Ian in their stolen meetings in night clubs, hotel lobbies, parks? "Nowhere, I guess," she said after a moment. "It must be nice to be married." She raised her eyes to Aunt Violet's and received the blue ray which had opened so many hearts, the transparent deep look which was no doubt some matter of the precise color of the iris and not as it always seemed—as it seemed to Sally—the removal of a wall, the opening up of a private intimacy, given to her alone.

She was moved. She walked over to one of the long windows and looked out. Because she was moved, the curve upwards of the meadows, the grove of oaks seemed incredibly green and brilliant as if they had just been created before her eyes, dripping with rain, and now illuminated by the peculiarly radiant sunlight. All this took a few seconds, as it took Violet a second to answer,

"That depends."

"You and Uncle Charles . . ." Sally's back was still turned. She did not know how to say what she wanted to say. "Well—you seem to have some sort of private magic. It's being in love, I suppose," she said ironically. "You're still in love, aren't you?" And now once more, turning to face her aunt, she attacked, she dominated. She was afraid of the moment which had just passed. In it she had forgotten Ian altogether. He might never have existed as she felt herself drawn down into the depth of

Violet's glance. This frightened her. She felt that she must hang on to Ian every second, every hour, or he might disappear.

"Are we?" The archness of Violet's tone suggested evasion. "I don't know. When you've been married nearly thirty years, you no longer ask yourself that question."

"What do you ask yourself?"

"Oh, I don't know, silly things—"

"Like what?"

But Violet at the moment could not think what she had meant to say. "I really must finish the flowers, now I have finished my drink. You might go and take a look —I thought I heard the gate click just now. It might be the post . . ."

And so, Sally thought, I am being dismissed. Grown-up people never would tell you the things you needed most to know. Go to your Ian, her Aunt Violet was saying, and leave me alone with my flowers, with this house which you desecrate with your untidiness, with your interruptions, with your very presence perhaps. Sally stood on the terrace watching the postman bicycle very slowly down the drive. She was upset. So far she had maintained her equilibrium where Ian was concerned by leaning towards him and against all the wishes of those close to her. Now suddenly she was being pushed towards him, she felt almost as if she had fallen down again, flat on her face, at the bottom of the stairs. The first had been a real fall, and she had hurt her knee. What have I hurt now, she wondered?

"Good morning, Miss. There's a letter for you"—the very young postman grinned—"There, I've put it on top."

"Oh thank you, thank you very much." Sally ran through the glass door, letting it swing shut behind her, flung down the rest of the mail and fled up the stairs with the letter in her hand. She both wanted to open it and didn't want to. She sat on the bed turning it over, feeling quite ill suddenly. What if? What if? But now she was lying on her stomach reading it, tasting the "Darling Sal" which crept through her blood like a liquor, like some wonderful drug which would give everything again its just proportion, like some inward sunlight, wholly healing. The rest of the letter was all about himself, about a radio program he would be on for the next three weeks as a substitute, about his chances for summer theatre jobs, about the vague possibility of a lead in a road company. "Don't do anything foolish," it ended. As if I could, she thought. She had waited for the letter with such passionate anxiety, with the attention of her whole person for so many days and nights, that now it seemed disappointing. It's Ian, I want, not his letters, she pushed her face into the pillow. Oh Ian . . . But in the disorder of the room, in her inward disorder, she could not at the moment even imagine his kisses. It was as if the letter had taken him one step farther away, not brought him closer at all. She sat for a long time with the silver frame in her hands trying to make his face real. But she was frightened when after this intense contemplation what rose behind her eyes was not his face at all, but Aunt Violet's. She slammed the silver frame down on the bed. "They won't get me," she said aloud, "they won't." She turned the knob on the radio to let some loud music blot out everything else. It came as it always did, suddenly out of the air, this loud crazy sound of love and self-pity. Sally abandoned herself to it this time without caring whether the house hated it or not.

Downstairs, satisfied at last with the spiky symmetrical mass of foxglove and larkspur and Canterbury bells, Violet winced as the music upstairs took possession again. Just when it seemed as if Sally might be adapting herself a little, slightly tamed, this sort of thing always happened. And Violet went out into the garden to find Charles. Now the sun was out, everything steamed; waves of mist rose up from the grass.

"Oh, Charles, there you are!" she cried, as if she had been looking for him for ages.

"I've been here for hours," he said. "Look at this bed. Better, eh?"

"It's lovely," she said, looking vague.

Charles stuck his spade in upright. "You're not paying attention. If you looked at what I've done, you'd realize that I've nearly finished transplanting the iris. Here I slave away . . ." he began to scold her, all the time looking at her with intense pleasure, as if he had really been a long way off and she had found him.

"Sally has finally got her letter." She glanced up at the square windows at the top of the house. Even from here one could hear the distant throbbing.

"Well, maybe then we'll have some peace. And now for Heaven's sake, pay attention to me for a few minutes."

Violet was not to be distracted. "Charles," she said earnestly, "perhaps we should invite someone here. Don't you think it might help?"

"Here, you intolerable woman, take my arm and come for a walk. If we have to talk about Sally, a subject of which I am heartily tired, let's do it at least in pleasant surroundings." He prodded her elbow.

"But it is splendid about the iris," she said, with maddening inconsequence, refusing to budge. "You really have done wonders, Charles," she said peering now intently at the dug-up bed and the fat gnarled roots scattered about.

"I don't want to be disturbed. There's too much to do, Violet. And I thought this summer was to be peace and quiet and a chance to get thoroughly settled."

99

So they talked, still standing by the bed, picking up and dropping the threads, at entire cross-purposes, and in entire communion.

It was Sally's turn to sit in the embrasure of the window and look down into the garden. The voices broke into laughter suddenly, then murmured together. She went back to turn off the radio. It was as if some intimate music which she could just barely catch were coming from the garden, and the interval between Aunt Violet, leaning on a parasol, and Uncle Charles beside her, filling his pipe, were a musical interval. She looked down, fascinated. The two figures, vertical in the midst of the horizontal lawn, with small exact shadows lying before them, gave the whole scene focus. She saw Uncle Charles put an arm round Aunt Violet's shoulders in such a way that she wondered if he were asking forgiveness for something; she wondered what tender words accompanied the gesture.

"I have been wondering," Charles was saying at that moment, "whether pigs mightn't be a good idea. There are those old stables—"

"But Charles, the smell!" Violet protested. "Surely not so near the house!"

At that second, aware that the radio had been turned off, they both looked up. Sally withdrew quickly without making a sign, then realized this made it look as if she had been really spying. She felt miserably lonely.

"She watches us," Charles said softly. "Whatever do you suppose she's thinking?" Again he looked up at the blank window. The sense that they had been watched from above, perhaps for some time, unnerved him.

"She has gathered that we are still very much in love."

"Whatever makes her think that?" Charles was cross. He felt intruded upon, but also, and this surprised him, somehow pleased.

"What?"

"Well, whatever she thinks." He was unwilling to repeat the words aloud.

"Aren't we?" Violet was enjoying herself immensely.

"All you ever think about at night is bats." Charles refused to be led on. He did not approve of putting his sentiments into words. It was inappropriate and embarrassing.

"And all you ever think about is sleep."

"All right," he said. And then, to change the subject, he added, "She displaces too much atmosphere, for me, that little object."

"Yes," Violet sighed, "she came and interrupted me fearfully while I was doing the flowers."

On this, their talk lapsed, while each pursued his own thoughts. They walked slowly, arm in arm up the long avenue to the gate and back again. The stones of the house had turned a dull gold as they dried in the sun. There was everywhere the smell of earth and hay and Violet was thinking, Why can't she feel this? Why doesn't it speak to her? and she was thinking, How have we failed?

For Sally had wanted to talk, perhaps to confide, and

Violet, determined to get the flowers done, to progress through the day without breaking its rhythm (eleven in the morning was not a time for heart-to-heart talks), had not responded, not really. She had thought of the house, of the garden, of making this new life with Charles seem real, as her job of this summer. She did not want to be distracted, yet that morning, meeting Sally's eyes, so young and defiant, so hungry for love, she had had to face the fact that only one thing was really important, to make this summer flower for her niece. It would have to be taken on, all this. She could not evade it any longer.

"I think we've let her alone too much, Charles. She may not seem to, but she really wants to be looked out for. I wonder what we might invent?" Violet said, looking off at the purple hills back of the house, "We might go to the meadows and see if the wild strawberries are any good this year?" It was a question.

"Are there strawberries in the meadows?"

It always amazed Violet to remember that Charles had no memories of life here. "Of course," she said, "hadn't I told you?" For to her the image was so very clear; Barbie and she and Nanny sitting under a bush having a picnic tea, the heat and the flies, and Nanny's fear of the cows, and the fun of splashing through the brook. Filled with these memories, she looked up at Charles by her side (she had not known he existed then) and saw him as he had first appeared on horseback, riding over with neighbors for tea, the joy that sprang out where he walked, the impression he made of clean beautiful power, so she who was always the leader and the center had felt intolerably shy, as if he must see her heart beating too fast under the white voile dress with a blue sash, must guess the terrible desire she felt to touch his head, to feel its shape with her hands.

"Do you remember the dress I wore when you rode over that first day?"

"Of course not," Charles chuckled. "Was it nice?"

"You never remember anything." She was suddenly sad that he did not remember.

"I remember thinking you were about the prettiest girl I had ever seen," he said to placate her.

"Never mind, darling, don't be polite." She took his arm. "Good Heavens, you must have got wet through in that rain. You should have changed. Charles, you must be more careful," she said feeling the damp all the way up his arm anxiously, "you'll get rheumatism in your shoulder again."

"I'm not as old as all that," he said crossly. "I'm perfectly all right." It was torn out of him, the little sharp phrase. So he too minded, he too felt the veil being slowly drawn over the brilliance of his physical being. Violet said nothing, letting him go up the steps alone, for suddenly she could not bear the thought of their growing old, of their dying. It seemed cruel that this house would go on, that the trees would outlive them and every spring seem young again, but they would grow old, would change, were changing, so that time had suddenly begun to accelerate in a frightening way,

103

and she felt, standing still on the terrace that she was slowly but implacably being pulled away from all this, that she was on a moving stairway while everything else, the sun, the steps, the great bowl of hills that sheltered the house, remained stationary. Here where the past always flowed so gently into the present that they seemed beautifully woven together, it had never occurred to Violet so sharply before, that there was also the future, that they were not standing still, that little by little the future was eating into the past, into the present, and would finally devour them both.

After lunch they set out, carrying baskets and a small tin pail, and walking in single file, Charles in the lead, then Sally in her blue jeans, shirttails tucked in (was this a gesture of conciliation?), and finally Violet wearing a large straw hat, for her delicate skin could not stand the sun. They passed into the chill green gloom just behind the house; the empty stables where nettles, monstrously healthy, grew right up between the shafts of an old cart. They passed into the hot sunlight reflected off the brick wall of the garden, then through a glade of small trees to the shallow brown brook. Charles splashed through it happily. Sally, who had been whistling *La Vie en Rose,* stopped short. She had been dreamily contented, contented to be a passive member of the trio, to go wherever Uncle Charles led and for once not to think, even about Ian.

But she could not wade in her brogues. They would be ruined. Once again she was the stranger, who broke the rhythm, this time in spite of herself. Aunt Violet, just behind her, did not understand her hesitation.

"It's my shoes," she explained. "I'll have to take them off."

Sitting down, she watched Aunt Violet wade unconcernedly through the shallow brown water, flowing swiftly over flat stones. "I'll catch up!" she called. She felt hot and uncomfortable. These people seemed entirely adapted to their surroundings, wearing shoes which water did not hurt, for instance. She got up clumsily, balancing her pail in one hand and her shoes and socks in the other, and almost fell as her foot slipped on a stone. Then she was safely across, wrenching the socks over her wet feet.

Uncle Charles and Aunt Violet were far ahead now and she ran to catch up. It was a little thing, this awkwardness of a moment, yet it had spoiled her sense of comfort and pleasure. She felt subtly put in the wrong. This would have been a satisfaction even two days ago; now, since Ian's letter, it bothered her. For his letter instead of bringing him closer had, in a queer way, set her adrift. Now she was, she felt, entirely alone. So she ran desperately to catch up, as if she could find some mooring when she reached the two figures, walking so steadily off into the sunlight.

They were emerging into open fields, and the full blaze beat down. The soft turf was full of holes where the cows had stood and Sally stumbled several times, annoyed by her awkwardness. Did "they" never stumble? When they had come out in the third pasture, Aunt Violet turned.

"Here we are!" Then noticing her niece's flushed face, "Don't hurry, child. It's far too hot."

Sally came to a halt by her aunt, panting, brushing the gnats out of her eyes, and for the first time looked around. The house was out of sight. They were entirely surrounded by fields, broken up by rather scraggly hedges, tall enough to close in the view. They could not see anything near-by except their own green enclosure, but, off in the distance, the deep purple humps of the hills seemed much closer than they did from the house. High up in the sky there was a continual twittering.

"Larks," Aunt Violet said, watching Sally's frown, obviously puzzled because she could not see the bird in the blue above them.

The glare made Sally's eyes hurt. She could feel the sweat down her back and the shirt clinging to her shoulders. She did not look at Aunt Violet because she was quite sure that her aunt must look cool and delightful and perfectly at home in these surroundings, as she did everywhere. She looked down instead, grateful for the tuft of buttercups, one thing at least which she did recognize and could name.

"Buttercups," she said, pleased.

"There are masses of berries," Uncle Charles shouted. He was already systematically at work, on his knees. "Come on and get to work, you lazy women!"

For a half-hour they picked with silent, sleepy concentration. Very slowly Sally lost her sense of awkwardness and began to enjoy trying to outpick Uncle Charles; they were at opposite sides of a patch, moving towards each other. Aunt Violet had started at the far end of the field, by herself. Every now and then Sally straightened up, lit a cigarette, stretched and gave herself the secret pleasure of looking at her aunt. The large straw hat, floppy, tied under her chin with a pale blue scarf, gave her a charmingly old-fashioned look. She was, Sally decided, far away somewhere in the past, in a time, she thought with a pang, when I wasn't even born. She was wholly absorbed like a child, not to be touched. And this impression of Sally's was quite true, for picking wild strawberries was such a summer tradition of the house that Aunt Violet was dreamily half-consciously re-enacting innumerable summers, listening to the change of note as the little berries first slowly covered the bottom of the empty basket and then plopped down on each other silently as the second layer began.

The air seemed full of birds. Every hedge broke into

song, first one and then another; small birds swooped out and chattered, and always overhead there was the high sweet twittering of the invisible larks.

"Charles, your patch is much better than mine!" Sally watched his big hand gather in what looked like dozens of little strawberries in one quick skilful gesture.

"It's all in the game," he answered without looking up. And she felt how it was a game and Charles would take games seriously and have to win. She had cared about winning at first, glad to have this definite thing to do, but now she did not care at all. A kind of ease welled up inside her. She recognized it as The Spell. In a moment, if she did not take care, she would be happy, she would belong. . . .

Whenever this happened, she knew she must attack, show to herself and to them that she was not in any way a real part of life here. At college she had revolted in the same way against Miss Park's brilliant lectures on sociology, against the atmosphere at Vassar of teaching responsibility, of teaching usefulness. She had revolted because she was in love with Ian who had nothing to do with all this, and about whom she had always a vague sense of guilt. She had reached outside her own world to find her love, and that had made it all the more inviolable, secret, and hers. Now as she looked for an arm against the spell of the sun and the strawberries and Charles's intent self beside her, Miss Park's lectures came to her aid.

"It's all very well," she said in such a loud and argumentative tone that Charles stopped picking.

"What's all very well?" he asked, startled again by the fierceness of her gaze, so out of place.

"All this," she looked around with a slightly remote, an indulgent air, looked down at Aunt Violet, looked off to the humped purple hills. "But what does it all mean?"

Charles was puzzled. For the first time he noticed that the sun was very hot on the top of his head, and that his knees were very stiff indeed.

"You know," he said, panting a little as he straightened up, "we'd better sit down in the shade for a bit, call a break, what?"

He stretched himself out comfortably under the hedge and Sally sat down beside him, the cigarette hanging out of her mouth in a way he particularly disliked.

"Come and rest, Aunt Violet!" she called without taking the cigarette out of her mouth.

"No thanks." Violet didn't lift her head. She was much too involved in this moment to walk all that way, and besides she did not want to talk. The afternoon had taken on the color of eternity, as her afternoons as a child had done. It was a whole piece of time without beginning or end, going back as far as memory did, enclosing her like a dream. She was happy.

"Now what on earth are you getting at?" Charles asked, carefully tamping the tobacco down in his pipe. Sally found herself always watching his neat way of doing things, as if one could read in the way he folded up his tobacco pouch the very essence of the man.

"Well"—she forced herself to make the point—"I mean

this life here. It flows along. You go out with Cammaert. Aunt Violet does the flowers. There is the house always to be thinking of—but what does it all mean?" she said almost crossly, because it was an effort to say it at all.

"You know," he lounged comfortably beside her, not at all disturbed, "I've never asked myself that question. You see, I was forced to retire rather younger than is usual by the Burma business—and well—here we are." He looked over at her with a kindly half-amused look, as if she were a child, Sally thought.

"What does the house mean then? What is it all about, this tradition, this big house set down in the midst of the country? Surely the life such things represent doesn't exist any more? Does it?" The more she tried to pin down what had been in her mind, the more baffled she felt. Miss Park and Vassar seemed infinitely remote, though she begged them inwardly to come to her aid. "You said yourself you didn't much like it." She was ashamed of herself for this lapse into what Miss Park would call an Ad Hominem argument.

"Did I?" Charles sat up, indignant. "Whenever did I say that?"

"Oh," Sally pulled up a piece of grass and looked at it, "the other day when we were walking down the drive. You said not to tell Violet."

The antagonism he felt excited Charles. For someone so young Sally had an amazing power of disconcerting him, and he jabbed back like a very young man.

"What about your fiance? What's going to be the

meaning of your life and his, eh?" He said it sharply as one parries a real thrust.

"I hate you." Sally turned her face away to hide the tears which she would not, would not allow to fall, and tearing up another tuft of grass, "You're mean."

"You've got to take as good as you give."

There was now a silence. If Sally had wanted to break the spell, she had succeeded beautifully. Her fists were clenched in her pockets. She would have liked to hit Charles.

"I love him," she said through the tears which now would not be forced back. "Leave me alone."

Charles was not a man whom tears irritated. Violet never cried; he had little experience of tears, and he was very much upset now. He reached over to put his hand on the small tear-stained fist. "You do make it hard for us, you know—"

"I know," she was sobbing now, great ugly sobs, "I can't h—h—help it."

When Violet looked up she saw a blur which seemed to be Charles and Sally embracing. The eternity of the afternoon split open to exactly half past three, for for some reason she looked at her watch. She became exactly fifty-two years old, and the sharpness of her suffering exactly matched the happiness she had experienced a moment before. But it's not possible, she thought, wishing for once that she did wear glasses.

A few seconds later she realized that Sally was in tears and that Charles had been comforting her, that was all. But the initial shock had been too great and she could not get it out of her consciousness like some vivid dream which colors the whole of a day, and even affects one's attitude to people who have appeared in it quite unlike their real selves.

"It's really too hot," she said, coming up to where they sat. "We'd better get back to the house." She was annoyed with herself for feeling embarrassed.

"Come along, old girl." Charles got up with amazing lightness and pulled Sally to her feet by her two wrists, then turned to Violet and met her clear gaze unabashed. "We've done rather well as a matter of fact," he said. Violet saw that he meant the strawberries, as he held out the two pails.

"Look!" She showed her nearly full basket and triumphed.

The procession formed itself again, Charles taking the lead, Violet following him, and Sally, disheveled, ashamed of herself, straggling behind, a cigarette hanging from her lips. Because she had cried, Charles would feel he had some real relationship with her now. Especially as she had to admit that it had been a comfort to lean against his shoulder, an immense comfort. This, she knew, was even more dangerous. For she could handle what he might think of her, she could withdraw. But she could not handle what she might feel herself. She had not said what she meant about the house. It had sprung out of a desire to attack, to break the spell, but now she felt it had been after all a real question, a major question. She was walking slowly, absorbed in these thoughts, looking down at the grass and the buttercups. She hardly noticed how far behind she was. When she lifted her head she saw Uncle Charles and Aunt Violet now from a great distance as if they were children, sauntering along, absorbed in the pleasures of the moment, impervious to imminent war, to the fall of empires, as children are, entirely enclosed in their private life, it seemed. What did Charles think about Burma? Had he been angry when he was driven out, or only sad because the teak, as he had explained to her, was a complicated business and the Burmese did not have the trained people to take over? Was he really as detached, as magnanimous as he seemed?

Uncle Charles took the basket from his wife's arm. They feel nothing passionately except themselves, Sally decided. They have no convictions. They are useless people like the people in Chekhov, she decided, relieved to have defined them and so, in a sense, got rid of them as presences who had the power of putting her in the wrong continually, of treating her as a wayward child.

At least Ian earns his living—part of the time, she thought, walking quickly now, her head high. Yes, she thought, Ian earns as much as five hundred a week when he has a job. Yes.

She caught up with them, just as they had crossed the stream, and turned to wait for her. Sally stood looking across as if what flowed between them here was more than the shallow brook, time itself, a wholly different vision of life, and there could be no crossing over.

Charles wondered why she was standing there like a little stubborn foal, staring as if she saw something she might shy at.

"Come along," he said, "and be careful of the stones —they're slippery," for he was still feeling solicitous.

Obediently, for it did not matter, she sat down and took off her shoes and socks, this time without hurrying, as if she were in command. How different from her clumsiness and panic on the way over! She rolled her socks neatly into her shoes, held them in one hand by the strings and her pail in the other. She felt graceful and at ease and enjoyed the delicious coolness of the water flowing over her bare feet.

She would have liked to stay there and paddle about, and with something of this in her mind, perhaps to tell them to go along, she lifted her head. It happened that her eyes met Aunt Violet's and for the second time the clear blue gaze touched her, reached down to the most secret part of herself.

This time Violet knew very well what she was doing. She was looking, with a sense of Sally's reality as a person and not just a child, and judging her as one judges a real antagonist. It was a powerful collision.

And then, as if they had been playing that game where the players lock hands and try to throw each other off balance, the locked glance slipped as Sally grasped wildly into the air and fell plunk into the water, the pail of strawberries emptied out and bobbing away. It took Charles half a second to run in and lift her out, still clinging to her shoes which she had managed to keep clear of the water.

"You do fall down rather a lot," Charles said, smiling broadly at the dripping little figure which looked so angrily and fiercely at him.

"Don't tease her, Charles." Violet could afford to be magnanimous.

"As long as I did fall you should have let me enjoy lying in the brook. It felt lovely," Sally said harshly. "You would come and pull me out. You would have to do that." She ran off down the path ahead of them in her bare feet, the shoes bobbing up and down clumsily in her hand.

When they got back to the house, Sally had disappeared. There was no sound, Violet noticed, as she stopped on the landing wondering if she could go up to Sally's room, and deciding against it. Charles had been rather miffed at being treated so roughly.

She felt tired as if she were on the brink of a journey she did not want at all to make. Or was it only the journey back into the angular present from the gentle flow of the past? She felt without reasoning that the afternoon had had an imminent quality, like one of those immensely placid summer days that are called weather breeders.

And then she remembered that some nice dull acquaintances from a domain twenty miles away were coming to tea. It would be a good thing, perhaps, if Sally for once conformed and changed into a dress. Later she would go up and tell her so. Later, not now. Now she would lie down on the great bed and close her eyes, and not think of anything. But is there a cake? Violet thought, slipping into a dressing gown.

Sally was sitting in the embrasure of the window, her arms clasped round her knees. She was shivering. Always the house felt cold when one came in from out of doors, and even her sweater pulled up round her chin did not stop the shiver. But she sat there, looking out at the grove of oaks and the familiar sweep of the hill as she had looked at them from the window of the library the day she had talked to Aunt Violet when she was arranging the flowers. The landscape which she refused usually to look at, which was simply there, part of all that she would not accept, nor feel, rested her now. It was queerly consoling. It set a bound, a rim to the intense loneliness, whereas the house always seemed like a shell, a huge, silent shell which threatened to engulf her because she had no way to fill it,

116

because she would have no part of the life inside it, such as it was.

I am suffering from something, she thought, but I do not know what it is. Her anger against Charles, her passionate tears, her passionate assertion of her love for Ian—none of it seemed real. What seemed real was Aunt Violet alone in the far end of the pasture, Aunt Violet staring at her with so deep a judging look at the brook. I've been wounded, but I don't know where, she thought. Where? she asked herself, getting up quickly and staring into the mirror. Her own eyes looked bold and opaque to her now. There was no look in them at all. So what had Aunt Violet seen which made the black pupils open like a shutter in the clear blue iris? It was as if she had taken a photograph of a secret. Sally felt exposed, a little frightened. I have given something away, she thought, but I don't know what it is.

Very slowly she began a letter to Ian as if this might help. "I am becoming so stupid here for lack of any real life, because I miss you so terribly all the time, that today I cried and also fell into a brook when we came back from picking strawberries—" but what would Ian know of picking strawberries? How could she possibly communicate with him? Or tell him? She had got no further, but was still sitting on the edge of the bed, sucking her pen in a rather childish hypnotized way when Aunt Violet knocked.

"May I come in for a moment?" Violet was dismayed by the foreign look of her room which, she thought, resembled a limbo, clothes flung down on the floor, roses faded in their glass. "My dear child, I must get you some fresh flowers. Doesn't Maire ever tidy up for you? I must speak to her . . ." She stood with the wet jeans in her hand, plainly upset.

Sally had not moved. She sat on the edge of the bed, looking at her aunt with amusement and pleasure.

"Don't speak to Maire," she said finally while Aunt Violet fidgeted about, throwing the roses into the waste-basket with her free hand. "It's my fault, Aunt Violet —and do put down those horrible jeans."

Aunt Violet fended off the hand ready to take them from her. "I'll put them to dry in the kitchen. I came up because," she hesitated, spoke almost breathlessly as if she were afraid of a rebuff, "I thought you might like to change for tea. There are some people coming."

"What people?" Sally backed away against the chest of drawers.

"Oh, just the Desmonds. They have a place twenty miles away. They're rather dull, as a matter of fact. Charles will talk horses with them, and you and I," she said with an air of complicity, "will look as pretty as possible. They will eat a great deal— Good Heavens, I must go down and see about food!—They will ask to be shown the house." Violet had not meant to draw quite such a cruel portrait, but now she was enjoying herself, and enjoying Sally's softened air. "Do be a good child and help," she ended, drinking from Sally's eyes the wine of admiration, of respect, of love which could make her beauty shine even now. She could feel the aura she had missed like a tangible luminosity around her. And it did not matter very much to Violet, it never had, from whom this light came, as long as it came from someone, as long as she was not without it.

"All right"—Sally sounded as if she were granting half a kingdom to a Queen—"I'll put on a dress."

And Violet's smile then, so unexpectedly radiant, was worth half Sally's kingdom. She went off, moving lightly across the ballroom, as if she were suddenly ten years younger. The only thing she had wanted, at times rather desperately, from Sally, was recognition. Now, slightly ashamed of herself, she felt, I exist again. What a queer thing!

Sally dressed, conscious of this new desire to please which was driving her beyond all her resolutions. I'll be pretty, she thought grimly, if it kills me. And then, quite suddenly, she laughed. After all, why not yield to charm as long as one didn't believe in it, as long as she could hang on to her defined conception of her aunt as a useless person with no purpose?

Why not give people what they wanted? Mightn't this be an even better way of keeping oneself intact? And how much pleasanter and easier life would become! I've been a fool, she thought, a silly little fool.

She had deliberately waited until she heard the car drive up, so she came down the main flight of stairs as the Desmonds were entering the great hall from the terrace. They were four: a tweedy gentleman in a suit like Bernard Shaw's with rolled woolen socks to the knee; a dowdy woman with a surprised look dressed in a Liberty print with a choker of amber beads which did not match the pinks and yellows of the dress; and two awkward, red-faced, very pretty girls in gray flannel suits. They brought with them an atmosphere which Sally felt at once as wholly different from her uncle's and aunt's and—she decided—saner. Or was it only duller? They shook hands with no apparent interest in her, except for Mr. Desmond's fleeting look of astonishment, and concentrated at once upon the house as if it were a thoroughbred horse whose points must be completely appreciated before they could settle down.

"Yes—quite—I see," Mr. Desmond nodded as Charles pointed out the cornices, the ceiling, and no one but Sally seemed to notice or care that the wallpaper was peeling off along one wall and hanging down in strips. They commented upon the Victorian additions. They stood, a compact group, and surveyed the staircase, Mrs. Desmond pursing her lips appreciatively. Then they turned to the wall of portraits.

Angus Desmond froze into attention like a pointing dog and then beat his temple with one finger, as if he could pin down a memory hidden there, as he adumbrated Violet's comments, with curious facts of his own, about Sarah St. Leger. "Outside the pattern, eh, Mrs. Gordon?" and passing on to a rather dim face, he paused, "Oh yes, oh yes—the sister of my great-grandfather's first wife, isn't it? What was her name now?" the impatient finger tapped his temple again, "Elisabeth? Caroline? No, what am I saying? Charlotte, of course. Charlotte Dene—" and he looked at the face on the wall as if he had remembered her as a child, though she had died before he was born, "of a fall from a horse," he remembered. "It was rather mysterious, eh? Rumors, tales—" he added, and fell into somber reflection, upon, perhaps, the difficulties of historical accuracy in a country in which the simplest fact quickly grew from mouth to mouth into fantastic mythical splendor, violence or crime.

He then turned suddenly and looked Sally up and down as if he were measuring hers against the faces on the wall. "You can still see it, eh?" he said, smiling his pleasure as he bent towards Violet, "something in the eyes, that Dene look, a bit eccentric, what? There's a will there, not quite the usual thing . . ."

Sally blushed. She felt that her lipstick was out of place, that her severely cut yellow dress was too smart, that she was fatally outside the picture. And for the first time she looked up at the portraits of her ancestors on the wall with immense curiosity. What part of her came down from these, and what from ancestors of her father's? How were they intermingled?

The whole group moved now through the closed doors of the drawing room where, for some reason, Sally had not yet been. She stood on the threshold after they had passed through. In one corner an empty pedestal was covered with dust. Against the wall there were two long mirrors with delicate gilded frames and beneath them a sofa covered by a torn sheet. Otherwise the great high room was empty. The others had turned the corner and were out of sight. She heard something about the dining room,

"Victorian, of course. We don't know what to do with it," Violet was saying.

Still she stood on the threshold while the past flowed round her like an air current, assailed her nerves like a draught, not warm and enfolding like Violet's experience of it in the field, but frightening, dilapidated, inescapable, a weight. Why had that Charlotte Dene fallen from her horse? What did Mr. Desmond mean by "eccentric"? Were her people not like other people? Was there madness here? Is that what Charles feels about the house, she wondered?

"What are you doing there?" Charles asked, coming towards her purposefully across the long empty floor. "I must say, you're looking very charming, Sally," he said, taking one of her hands and kissing it, as if such a gesture were the most natural he could imagine. "Come and see the dining room. There's gloom for you," he added and chuckled.

"But I don't want gloom," she said, walking very slowly and carefully after him as if he were tracing a path for her through walls of water, through crushing walls of some sort. "It frightens me here."

At this moment the sun burst through the clouds and inundated the whole huge empty space with warm light. Sally could have had no idea how brilliant it made her in her yellow dress, how present.

"You bring a new world—fresh air—" Charles heard himself saying, too late. The bright mocking eyes lifted and met his.

"It makes you feel romantic, but it makes me feel sad —and—scared," Sally shivered.

Then they turned the corner, went through a closed door and into a room which seemed devoured by the darkness of the leaves screening every window, a room painted a dull mauve, a horrible room with a dusty round table in the middle and a hideous mantel over the fireplace.

"Too bad," Angus Desmond was saying. He looked really grieved.

"Of course there's no money to do anything about it now," Violet sighed. "Come along, we'll catch cold here. It's so damp. All the leaves."

She led the way and as she came to Sally, slipped an arm through hers, and drew her back through the empty spaces of the drawing room which was now all air and light it seemed, the walls having mysteriously withdrawn, as the two Denes walked arm in arm, silently back into the familiar furnished places.

Charles took the Desmonds up to the ballroom for a few moments while Violet settled down behind the tea table, her back to the long windows of the library. Sally sat down beside her, saying nothing. She did not know how to put her question. But it was as if all the Denes now were taking possession of her, as if she were being sucked back into the past, into something she would be but would have no choice about being, the trick of a mouth or nose, some deep insecurity or slip of character which suggested that she was, and had always been, in peril.

"Aunt Violet," she asked, clasping her hands tight over her knees, trying to frame the question, "are the Denes queer in some way?"

"Whatever do you mean, darling? Of course not. We're just an average Anglo-Irish family, you know, nothing special . . ."

"What did Mr. Desmond mean then about eccentric?"

Aunt Violet pondered this, "We've gone our own way, I suppose, not been quite as much a part of the country as the Desmonds, for instance. There have been a couple of painters; your great-aunt Arabella ran away with an Italian Count—the usual sort of thing. You needn't look so anxious."

"Really? That's all?" Sally asked, half disappointed now, so strong had her sense of something hidden become, just now, on the threshold of the empty drawing room.

"Yes, why?"

"Has it ever been a happy house, Aunt Violet?"

The question took Violet completely by surprise. For her the very perfume of happiness rose from the house— security, childhood, love, protection—it was everything good and dear. Sally saw the tears of surprise, the hurt in the clear blue eyes, and suffered. "Oh, I shouldn't have said it," she murmured. She wanted very much to take the hand that lay, so abandoned in her aunt's lap, to take it and kiss it, as Uncle Charles had so easily, it seemed, kissed hers. But it was impossible to make this gesture.

"No reason, Sally, why you shouldn't say it. I know you're not happy here. That has been clear enough," she added drily.

They heard the voices on the stairs, and there was no time to mend what seemed now a real wound.

Even a day ago such a remark from her aunt would have been a triumph, would have proved that she was resisting successfully, that she had succeeded in remaining a prisoner here, not a member of the family. Now the wound (but she did not know where it was) ached. She felt miserable, an outcast. She had brought tears to those magical blue eyes—this gave her a queer kind of satisfaction. But now she was interrupted in all her thoughts. She must pass the muffins and the jam and the plates and napkins. Tea was a formidable meal. At intervals Maire appeared, her red hands trembling a little, with another plate of sandwiches, more bread and butter, finally the cake. The Desmonds ate with quiet competence, passing their cups for more tea, settling down with an air of belonging which Sally envied. She found herself looking at the two girls speculatively —how did they live? What did they do? When she had passed things for what seemed hours, she sat down beside the prettier, the elder sister whose name was Daphne. "Do you ride a lot?" she asked. In the corner opposite, Uncle Charles and Mr. Desmond were deep in some technical matter about the last meet. Violet seemed stranded among the teapots, wearing a faint absent-minded smile.

"Oh yes, every day." Daphne smiled a quick, shy smile. "You must come over. I'm sure your uncle will bring you."

"I suppose you jump too?"

This seemed to amuse Mary, the younger sister. She giggled. "Well, you see," Daphne explained kindly, "you can't hunt without jumping, very well."

"And in the winter do you go to school or college?" For Sally realized that she could never hold up her end in a conversation about horses.

The two sisters exchanged a look. "Only frightfully clever girls go to college," Daphne explained. "I did go to a boarding school in England for three years. It was awful."

"I refused to go," Mary said. "What's the use of stuffing yourself with a lot of knowledge?"

Daphne looked at her sister with an amused look. "Even our governess gave Mary up two years ago. She was always looking out of the window or worrying that her caterpillars needed fresh leaves. But she has a very good French accent (our governess was French), haven't you, Mary?"

"You've been to Paris then?" Sally asked, hoping at last to find some point of contact, for she had been taken to Paris when she was sixteen.

"Oh no," and Mary giggled again. "I've forgotten all my French anyway."

By every standard which Sally possessed except charm these two bland, amused, contented girls failed miserably. They seemed to her absurdly young and unsophis-

ticated, with their rather rough hands and heavy out-
door shoes. Had they either of them ever been in love,
she wondered? And if so, with whom?

"I suppose there are balls in the winter?" she couldn't
help asking, though perhaps it was rude to ask so many
questions. The thing was that if she didn't, they looked
down at their hands, incapable, it seemed, of curiosity
about her in return, or too shy to show it.

"Oh yes, in the Hols— Daphne's engaged to be married," Mary confided suddenly. "Her young man's at
Cambridge. He's studying boilers." This was evidently
a family joke as the girls exchanged a look of extreme
amusement.

"He's going to be an engineer," Daphne explained.
What she had, Sally decided, was the dignity of a person who knows exactly what she is about. It was im-
pressive.

"I'm engaged too," Sally heard herself saying, as if
this would place her. But she caught their surprised
look as they glanced at her hand and did not discover
a ring.

"What's your young man?" Mary asked. This was a
subject which did interest her, at last.

"He's an actor, not a famous one, but he's very tal-
ented." It sounded absolutely impossible. Sally was
quite aware of this and the implication of Daphne's
"Oh." "I suppose," Sally said, lifting her chin in a family gesture of which she was entirely unconscious,
"that I'm one of the eccentric Denes."

This paralysed the two girls completely. Luckily Aunt

Violet had caught the last remark and Sally's defiant air.

"So you're a Dene, are you?" she teased. "I thought you were a dyed-in-the-wool Philadelphia Calvert."

"An eccentric Dene what's more," Charles chimed in. He had been hoping for some time to extricate himself from Mr. Desmond on the subtleties of various horses he owned or had owned or had seen recently. Also he had been watching Sally's noble efforts at conversation with amused appreciation. It seemed to Charles that the three girls who sat now rather primly, embarrassed by the intervention of grownups into their conversation, looked absurdly, unbelievably young. Sally was blushing which enhanced her air of innocence. It hurt him in a queer way that they should be so young. At this moment his wife's beauty, which he had always taken for granted, appeared to him as fragile and precious as a cherry tree in full flower which would begin to fall at any moment, which was falling, the petals turning faintly brown—he wished suddenly that the Desmonds would leave. It was an irrational sense that time was passing, and that he could not afford to waste a second of it.

"She's got the Dene air," Mr. Desmond said with satisfaction. "Of course it's a new generation . . ." he added vaguely, with less enthusiasm. And then for the first time he looked at Sally as if she were a person and not a portrait on a wall. "I expect now that Mrs. Gordon is back your family will be coming over for the summers again?" he asked. "Is your mother well? I remember her," he said, tapping his temple again. "She was a

128

lovely girl, not a great beauty like her sister," he said with a gallant nod of his head and a smile at Violet, "but full of life. I can see her now, running across the avenue, laughing at something or other, followed by two or three young men. By the way, Mr. Gordon"—for this had reminded him of something—"will you be getting the tennis courts back into shape?"

"If I can get the farm on its feet and do something about lumber we might be able to afford that—all in due time . . ." Charles said in a businesslike way. Sally had had no time to answer about her mother and now they were off on the problems of the estate. She could relax. Her moment of fearful self-exposure was over. She was safe again.

They had all three been disturbed during the Desmonds' visit. This intrusion of strangers had torn open feelings which had perhaps been emerging but not recognized. Violet felt it quite absurd to have allowed what Sally said about the house to hurt her so much, but she had allowed it and now she watched her niece warily, this niece who had the power to make tears start in her eyes (Violet never cried, or almost never) just because she was not happy here. Sally was sitting on the arm of a chair swinging her foot and frowning. She would have liked to apologize for what she had said, but something in her withstood this capitulation—Ian, perhaps. She kept forcibly placing Ian between her aunt and herself, as a protection against the waves of emotion. Whatever is happening to me? Sally thought and suddenly got up and walked out of the room, without a word.

"Where are you off to, Sally? I was just going to mix a cocktail . . ." There was distress in Charles's voice and Violet caught it at once. She sensed in herself, in Sally, now in Charles a precipitation of the atmosphere and wished to ward it off.

"Let her go," she said quietly. "You'll make her feel like a prisoner. She did her duty very valiantly by the Desmonds, but she has to escape, you know, she's so afraid of being caught," and Violet laughed a gentle slightly superior laugh.

"Well, then"—Charles turned away—"I suppose we might as well dress before we have a drink."

Just then it thundered, and exactly as if someone had opened a sluice in the sky, a great sheet of rain poured down.

On their way upstairs Violet and Charles stopped on the landing. It was quite dark.

"Wherever did the storm come from?" Charles asked.

"It was perfectly serene an hour ago." This change without warning was upsetting, unsettling. It made him feel as if he didn't know where he was.

Violet shivered. "It would be too bad if we were in for a spell of rain."

"Nonsense. It's a just a thunderstorm." He turned up the stairs, but Violet sat down a minute on the window seat and peered out. The mountains were completely hidden; sitting there neither downstairs nor upstairs, alone, she felt marooned, isolated, in a kind of panic. What if Charles—Violet pushed away the dream-image of Charles and Sally locked in each other's arms in the meadow, and fled.

But Sally was not thinking of Charles. She was walking up and down in her room (Violet sitting at her dressing table heard the footsteps, back and forth, back and forth and dropped the stopper of a perfume bottle). Sally was wondering how she would ever face Violet again, how she could possibly bring herself to go down to dinner at all. She had taken out her best sweater, black cashmere embroidered with pearls and silver thread. She tried buttoning it up to her throat over the yellow dress and then she tried it open, all the time seeing herself through Violet's eyes, then as she suddenly admitted this to herself, she tore the sweater off. That was when she began to walk up and down, hugging her arms, as if she were in pain. I cannot let this happen, she thought, it is too queer and upsetting. She took the photograph of Ian brusquely from the dresser and stared at it as if she were looking at a stranger. For months the whole world of sensation had been bound up in his face; everything she saw which moved her at all was related to his image, so she had only to murmur his name to feel his touch on her arm. Here in this place which she had regarded as a prison, he was her freedom, her escape, her identity and—she saw now—her safety too. And what was happening that she could hold his picture in her hands, and feel nothing? If only we'd been lovers, she thought, I'd be all right. I'd be safe. It was her fault that they hadn't, that they had only reached a point of exaggerated devouring tenderness, meeting in public places, stealing each other's caresses as if they were criminals, in taxis, or in Central Park early in the morning, when the sky was suddenly bright green, just before sunrise. Sally was waiting for a final gift on his part, and he had not made it. He had not asked her to marry him. He had talked of it as something possible in the distant future— Oh Ian, why? she whispered. But all she felt was what it had been like to walk through the empty drawing room in the sunlight with Violet's arm through hers, the perfect pure intense bliss it had been. She could see the images of her life with Ian—Central Park—but she could not feel them any more. It was as if they lay behind a pane of glass, and only what was here now touched her skin like sunlight or rain.

But I do love him, she told herself grimly. He's all I have. Against everyone, against everything, he's what I am, even if it's wrong, a waste, nothing those Desmond girls could ever understand. She could not see why the idea of the Desmond girls came to her. Whatever did it matter what they thought? Or their father, or Uncle Charles, old-fashioned, simple, romantic people, all of them.

Was she in some way set apart then from all that was normal, good, simple, possible? For all she wanted was to bury herself in Violet, to shut out the whole world, and to be enclosed accepted once and for all, to love and to be passionately loved by Violet. This fact was so overwhelming that she sat down on her bed, quite unable to go down and to face the reality. She just waited until Charles's loud clanging on the gong forced her to face them again.

"We're celebrating," Charles said. He seemed rather excited.

"What?" Sally asked bluntly. She was grateful to Charles for being there, now that she couldn't lift her eyes to Violet's face, now that she was so utterly constricted and frozen by the strength of her feelings.

"The relief it is to be together again, the relief that the invaders have come and gone, examined us, given us an A for conduct, approved, eaten a huge tea and left us to ourselves . . ." Charles was laughing. Sally had never seen him like this, so gay and excited. "Here's your drink," he said, touching her hair lightly as he gave it to her. "We've had one. You did take a long time to put on a sweater. You didn't knit it, did you? You didn't sew on all those little pearls between tea and dinner?"

Sally laughed in spite of herself. One couldn't resist

Charles in such a mood and the last thing she wanted was to resist him. Anything which would stop for a moment the awfully deep thump of her heart, the insistent stifled beat as if it wanted to leap out of her chest, anything was a relief. She threw herself into his mood and soon they were laughing as they had never laughed before, daring each other to further nonsense. Violet withdrew from their game and watched it, and watched the rain pouring down outside.

Only when they had gone in to dinner did Sally finally dare to look at Violet, sitting so remote and composed across the table, framed in the candles. She caught that considering, judging, unsmiling glance and in a second all her excitement fell. It was the same look which had thrown her as she was crossing the brook, the look of an antagonist, but Sally did not recognize it as that. She thought it was because of what she had said about the house. She felt the blush creeping up her neck and quickly, quickly to hide it, blurted out what she had been holding inside her all the evening,

"Forgive me, Aunt Violet," she said, her fingers crumbling the bread beside her plate.

"Whatever for, Sally dear?" For Violet was utterly at sea.

"Well," Sally stammered, "I mean—about—what I said about the house. It's just . . ." but she couldn't go on. It would take a year to explain all she meant.

"You don't need to explain," Violet said kindly and turned to Charles to ask him to ring for Maire.

"What's all this?" Charles asked, sensing the tension.

"Nothing, darling." And then with unconscious cruelty she turned back to Sally, "What do you hear from Ian these days?"

As Sally talked about Ian, about his plans, a summer play which had fallen through, she felt as if she were building a house of cards, so unreal did it all sound even to her. "He doesn't write very good letters," she ended, "that's what's so awful. None of the real things can be said it seems to me," but Sally was not thinking of Ian now. "I hate words. They're barriers. They never tell the truth."

It was said with a kind of violence. Sally felt herself that the tone was exaggerated. It was as if now she couldn't do the simplest things naturally. And she wished Charles and Violet would leave her alone and play one of their own games, one of their teasing self-absorbed conversations which included her as the necessary audience, but asked nothing of her. As it was, she felt exposed by Charles's attentions, by Violet's silences. It seemed as if everything had subtly changed between them in the last few hours and Sally didn't know how to cope with it. After dinner she made a lame excuse about a headache and went to bed.

Lying in bed, listening to the rain, she imagined them playing chess and pretending to be cross, enclosed in their love. Much later she heard footsteps on the stairs, a low laugh more secret than any words, and thought, "They're going to bed."

135

The next morning what had looked like a mere thunderstorm had turned into a steady fine drizzle. "Here to stay," Annie said, rubbing her rheumatic knee. The clouds were caught in this pocket back of the hills and it would take a strong wind from the sea to blow them back again. Sally felt more like a prisoner than ever; the rain kept Charles in and she was lucky if she had ten minutes alone with Violet. Even then there was nothing to say or do. We're like ships caught in a lock, Sally thought. There was no escaping the house now. They were shut up together in the damp rooms, huddled round the fire in the library, muffled in sweaters and scarves, taking hot water bottles up to bed. Violet spent long hours at her petit point, remote, rather nervous if spoken to, perhaps depressed. Charles fidgeted, did accounts, went out covered in a heavy raincoat, came back, damp and irritable, paced the floors, insisted that Sally play checkers with him (a game she hated), and swore at the rain.

"At least," Violet consoled, "we're not swelteringly hot, Charles. It's much better than the rainy season in Burma."

"Is freezing to death in midsummer better than sweltering?" He turned to her, exasperated. "Listen to the wind!"

A shutter banged. The situation was deteriorating every minute. Sally decided that soon something would happen, anything, and that anything would be better than this.

Instead of drawing them together, this period of suspension threw them back each into his own obsessions and fantasies. Sally had the feeling sometimes that her aunt was engaged in some secret painful battle with herself. This was actually true. Violet was going through a period of self-hatred and self-abuse, what she called "one of my depressions." She felt that Sally wanted something of her which she was not prepared to give to anyone except her husband. Charles had withdrawn. Ever since the day of the Desmonds' call, Charles had been going through some phase, turning towards her only the dark side of his moon. Beside this withdrawal there was the weight of Sally's silent love. Violet felt exhausted by the intensity of these personal relations. She who had all her life moved among them as her special element, wanting to be loved, enjoying the magnetic currents set up between people, now realized that she was getting old. Or—was it the house? She had a curious feeling that all this bother was irrelevant. Possibly she had even loved

Charles all these years in the wrong way. Such thoughts, which attacked the very roots of her life, frightened her.

Charles, not understanding what was going on, blamed everything on the weather, for the last thing he wished was to analyse or examine himself. It was he now who sensed an intangible intimacy when he came into a room where Sally wandered around like a ghost and Violet sat, too still, reading or sewing. He could not imagine why he was so irritated with Violet, and Sally bewildered him. She flirted with him quite obviously when Violet was present, but avoided ever being alone with him and refused his invitations to come out. All this made him feel like a bear, some clumsy animal blundering about among women and women's inexplicable moods. He took to going out in spite of the rain. He felt queerly lonely.

Sally, speechless where her aunt was concerned, became so tense that the smallest gesture, lighting a cigarette for Violet, passing her a cup of coffee, took on passionate significance; her hand trembled; the coffee spilled into the saucer. She did not even know what she wanted from Violet—some absolute naked recognition? What? She was like a poet in the state of high excitement which precedes the work of writing, but Sally had no such outlet nor discipline. The intensity took her nowhere, but was reflected back all the time and she felt as if she were forced to live under a powerful electric bulb night and day. The idea of tidying her

room, of doing this one definite thing to please Aunt
Violet, came to her as an inspiration. In some senses it
was a ridiculously small act as a receptacle for so much
feeling. But Sally knew that its symbolic significance
was not small. Destroying the harmony of the room
which had been Violet's as a child, had been quite deliberate. She did everything not to feel its atmosphere,
used the dressing table as a desk, putting the candle-
sticks and mirror carelessly on the floor, left her clothes
on the chairs, unmade the bed by lying down on it and
pulling the pillows out of their cases, let books lie on
the floor among odd shoes. This untidiness had become
a habit. After a while she hardly noticed the mess. Now
she went upstairs and worked furiously to recreate the
room as it had been. Maire was astonished when she
came up to find it immaculately neat and Sally sitting in
the armchair by the window in a tailored suit as if she
were going out.

"You're not leaving, Miss Sally?" she said, alarmed
by these radical changes.

Sally laughed, "On the contrary, I'm staying," she
said. "Maire, be an angel and ask Aunt Violet to come
up, will you?" Sally asked, as Maire prepared to leave
with the slop pail. Sending a messenger was the only
possible way she would have dared invite Aunt Violet
here. Now she looked around with dismay. The room
had become a stage, but what would she say? How
would she behave? All the last days had been building
up to this moment. She envied Ian who would act out

what was going to happen like a scene (she had seen him do it). But I have to be myself, she thought, it's much harder.

"Why darling child, what a transformation," Violet said amused, delighted, a little touched. For Sally was standing by the window, apparently overcome with shyness, like a person who has planned an enormous surprise and now pretends it is nothing, nothing at all—but Sally was frowning, did not look up. "I must say, it's lovely to see it all neat. Now if it would only stop raining I could go out and pick you a marvelous bunch of flowers—"

"Yes," Sally said looking around the room, as if the lack of flowers was a mistake she had made. "Flowers— I didn't think of that. You always do, don't you? You treat flowers like people, miss them when they're not there."

"I don't know . . ." Violet came over to where Sally was standing and they both looked out at the rain. "Summer—the house—flowers are part of it. My mother loved them." She was standing quite close to Sally and Sally stood there waiting, waiting, wondering if her aunt could hear the awful deep thud of her heart, the thudding blows of it as if she were being beaten from inside.

"What does it mean?" Violet asked gently. "That you've decided to 'live' here after all?"

This was her chance to say all that had been pent up for so long. Sally knew it, saw it come and go, but could say nothing. "I don't know—I—" and she turned away quickly, because she could not bear to stand so close to Violet any longer, because she could do nothing, could not take her hand and kiss it as she so longed to do, could not cry out some desperate loud cry which would be heard across the implacable fact of separation, the fact that they were two people, that they could never be one.

"I guess I was just bored by the rain," Sally lied. She could hardly wait for Violet to leave, so that she could rehearse in her mind over and over again this scene she had not been able to play, invent all the words she had not been able to say, do the marvelous impossible act which telling the whole truth had become. If only she knew, Sally thought, if only she did, that's all I ask.

But of course Violet knew, would have liked to say something consoling, to do something kind and gentle to ease things for Sally, and knew also that anything she might do would hurt. But Violet had a profound instinctive dislike of probing into other peoples' feeling, analysing, dissecting. She had too much respect for Sally to be condescending. She picked up the photograph of Ian in its silver frame and looked at it thoughtfully,

"He's a handsome boy," she said, and then as if this had some relevance, "It will be all right, Sally. You'll see."

"Maybe." Sally was glad of a subject on which to fasten. "He acts all the time. I wish I could. You do too, of course. You're always acting. It's from self-protection,

I expect." Sally's tone was dry and detached. She did not look at her aunt.

"I expect so."

"But what are you really like inside?"

Violet was at the door. Her instinct was to withdraw, but something in Sally's look made her stay in spite of herself, made her try to answer in spite of her distaste for this kind of self-revelation.

"Full of self-doubt like everyone else. I'm not honest as you are, as your mother was—"

"Yes, Mother's honest, but she's awfully simple," Sally spoke with authority. She seemed quite sure of this, and it made Violet smile.

"Not as simple as all that. She was a pretty complicated difficult little girl, you know. Intense, like you."

"Is it bad to be intense? I can't help it. Things matter."

"Of course they do, but . . ." Violet hesitated. How not to hurt?

"But what?" Sally asked, almost belligerently. She felt miserable. We are getting further and further away from each other, she thought. Aunt Violet is withdrawing into her wisdom.

"Well"—Violet looked towards the windows and the grey misty sky—"it's hard to keep a sense of proportion for one thing."

"I know," Sally said, blushing now. These words went right to her heart. "It makes one feel like a mad person. Do you think I'm mad, Aunt Violet?" she asked anxiously.

"Darling, of course not. I think you're wonderfully young and imaginative and so maybe you see things that just aren't there." It was a most unsatisfactory answer.

"To me they are there," said Sally shortly.

"Yes," Violet said slowly, "I know." Should she try now to speak? She was still in the door, still on the way out, but now she turned and walked over to the window where Sally still stood, her hands clenched. Violet put a hand on the tense shoulder and looked at Sally gravely. "It's not easy for you, darling. I can't help you there. But do you know, would it be any comfort to know that it has meant a great deal to Charles and me to have you here? Have you any idea how you have lighted up the house? What a delight it is to see you beginning to be part of the family—we have no children. We were feeling a little lonely, I think—and old—"

"You have each other," Sally said out of her misery.

"Yes." Violet took Sally's hand as cold as ice in hers and looked at it for a moment before letting it fall. "We have each other, but having each other isn't a static affair, Sally. If there's real feeling, it never stays the same for very long. It's nourished or starved by all sorts of atmospheres and things. How shall I say it?" Violet paused and again looked out. "You nourish us. Any real exchange between the young and the old is nourishing. And no love is wasted, Sally, believe me."

This was more than Violet had meant to say and now she fled before Sally could answer, fled downstairs and into her bedroom. She felt as if she had been holding a torrent at bay, and now with the effort of this, the effort to do it gently, not brutally, she was trembling. She guessed that she herself had never felt for anyone what Sally felt for her and almost she envied the capacity for such obsessive concentration. Does Ian have any idea of the treasure he holds in his hands, she wondered? Violet was astonished to find that she felt quite miserable, in some way deprived because she was depriving, in some way starved because she could not feed Sally's passionate hunger. For the first time in her life she faced the fact that a woman might long to give passionate love to another woman. It did not shock her.

But the next morning Violet decided she would withdraw, give Sally time, give herself time. She would stay in bed. A batch of books had arrived from London. She would forget Charles and Sally; she would try to recapture the equilibrium which these last days had all but upset.

Charles was delighted. "We'll go to town," he announced to Sally. "You'll see the gathering of donkeys and donkey-carts. It's quite a sight."

Sally felt caught up in his elation, glad of the relief from tension, glad that Violet would not see her face for she had cried half the night, that intensity having found the rock against which it could break and release itself in a surf of tears. As she stood on the terrace and waited for Charles and the car, she looked up at the house and felt really like a prisoner making his escape. And once outside the gates, purring along up and down the green hills and past the rivers, the ruined castles, the tinkers' carts pulled up by the wayside, once away from the demesne, she could breathe freely again. Everything seemed normal and she could even wonder what had made her get into such a state. Her feeling for Violet unknotted itself and was diffused by the open spaces, and seemed quite unreal like a dream.

Later in the pub, where they drank lager, Sally tested out this change in herself by talking quite condescendingly about Violet, quite from above as if she were grown-up and Violet a mere child. They relaxed, she and Charles, into the sense of power that indulgent love may bring.

"Violet is bored, I expect," Charles said, rather smugly.

"She's never bored." Sally was on the defensive at once. "But she goes off on some spiral of her own, some inner spiral. She's just not there."

"Quite," said Charles. "What you can't know is that

she's always been surrounded, rather, I mean by people who admired her, young men and so forth. She lights up for people."

"It's her reason for existing—yes—"

"Do you think so? Is that it, eh?" Charles lit a cigarette, expansive. It was quite extraordinary how this young girl understood things. In some way it seemed that Sally was inside his feeling, not outside it—in some way he felt she had a right to speak.

"And yet the queer thing is, Charles, that she feels so much guilt about it—is always struggling against what she needs, despising herself for needing it. She talks so much about feeling old. It's ridiculous," said Sally with the authority of a lover.

"Of course you never saw her as she was," Charles said thoughtfully.

"She's more beautiful now," Sally said almost crossly. She could not bear to think she had not seen Violet then.

Charles was amused by this vehemence. "It's fun to have someone in the family to talk to. I don't often talk about Violet, you know."

"I know"—Sally smiled back at him quietly—"I'm glad too."

"When you first came, you seemed rather at bay. It was disconcerting."

Sally frowned. This came too close.

"I wanted to be loyal to Ian. He's all I've got."

"But I don't see why the two things are incompatible," Charles said gently, feeling her alarm. "Are they?"

"I can't explain. It's too complicated." This conversation which had begun so well was becoming too difficult. Sally looked at her watch. "Heavens, Charles, we'll be late for lunch!"

Charles sang silly songs all the way back. Once he slipped an arm across Sally's shoulders and gave her a hug, but it all seemed part of the song he was singing and she rather liked it. She felt safe with Charles. In some way they had become allies against Violet and Violet's moods, the enormous amount of atmosphere Violet displaced. When she was with him, Sally could think of Ian. It was a long time since this had been possible at all.

But Charles felt a pang of jealousy when he saw a letter from Ian on the hall table when they got back. He watched Sally tear it open and then run off upstairs, wondered what her look of surprise, of shock could mean.

It meant that Ian was asking if he could fly over for a weekend, and hardly said more than that. He asked Sally to cable if possible so that he could make plans—he would have a few days free in a little over a week. But Sally found that she could not answer this offhand without some thought—she was not quite sure that she wanted Ian to come, just now, just when things seemed to be smoothing out to a kind of happiness and peace. She found she dreaded having to feel so much, having to face the reality of what she had dreamed and set apart in a world of fantasy. At lunch she was absent-minded and Charles, guessing part of the reason, minded.

"I am sick and tired of this bloody weather," he said to Violet, bursting in on her just as she was about to take a nap.

"Didn't you have a good morning with Sally?" Violet asked.

"Yes, I suppose so. Now she's had a letter from Ian. It's upset her," Charles said crossly.

"Oh." Violet considered this and considered him, smoking moodily in the straight chair by her bed. "Sally's got her own life, you know, darling. She's not our possession."

"I never said she was."

"No, that's true, you didn't—but"—Violet smiled carefully—"you're behaving rather as if she was. Is that quite wise?"

"I don't know what you're talking about."

"All right then, let me read in peace."

Sally, Violet thought, is at the place in her life where without being aware of it, she is like lightning that may strike anywhere. She's a bolt of life. In the last five minutes it had become crystal clear to Violet that her queer vision of Charles and Sally in each other's arms had had a partial truth in it. Then she looked around the high spacious room, and at the rain outside. They were all three losing their sense of proportion in the rain, and she for one would hold on to hers. So she forced herself to read, until she could lie down and sleep for an hour. Tomorrow, she told herself, I shall think all this out.

Tomorrow the sun may be out and we shall all be different.

But the minute Charles came in that night, Violet sensed that something had happened. What? She had not been a witness to the evening, but she sensed its atmosphere at once.

Sally and Charles had had a long talk about Sarah St. Leger. Sally, unable to come to a decision about Ian, had thrown herself with relief into Charles's expansive flattering mood. She plied him with questions and he foraged around in the desk happily to bring out a photograph of another painting of Sarah, dressed in black, her hair pulled back tight from the round full forehead, an air of implacable authority and willed kindness in the large eyes which Sally found repulsive. There was also an engraving, rather crude, of Sarah dispensing soup to an emaciated group of sufferers from the Famine.

"I don't think I should have liked Sarah," Sally said decidedly, "she was righteous wasn't she? She never doubted herself."

Would she have felt this three weeks ago? Wouldn't Sarah St. Leger three weeks ago have been the one person she was searching for in the past of the house? She after all had had a social conscience. The words came to Sally's mind like curiosities from another world. I'm changing, she thought, with panic. I'm no longer the same.

"But," she said turning to Charles, "she does add something to the history of the house, doesn't she? I guess it's big enough to contain all kinds of life—a cosmos."

Charles smiled. "A cosmos sounds a bit exaggerated."

"Americans like big words," and Sally laughed at her former self. "You're quite right, Charles. It's just an old house lost in the green—that's all it needs to be. Oh dear," she sighed, "there I go again, no sense of proportion as Aunt Violet would say."

"People with no sense of proportion get things done," Charles answered, enjoying the argument and Sally's quick response.

Sally met the amused regard in his eyes. It was nice to be admired. It made her feel set up, grown-up, not clumsy as she always did with Violet. She did not need or want to be one with Charles, so she was not afraid. Not even when he closed his strong warm hand over hers. It seemed natural, the pact that sealed a good day.

But to Charles this gesture had acted as an explosion of life. This was not love or anything like it, but only a way to recapture his sense of himself. Violet would receive the full impact, not Sally.

She felt it at once when he came in, the physical triumph in him. She felt it later in the return of a kind of violence, almost brutal in its self-absorption. He made love to her as if she weren't there, as if he were battling some unknown antagonist, perhaps time. It was as if he were saying "Hurry, hurry, we'll be dead before"— what? What he meant was that he had to prove himself again with a new person to be reassured, and that for a while Violet would have to be a lightning conductor.

Violet knew this mood. It had always been the first warning of a love affair.

And now she was afraid for herself, for Charles (would he be hurt?), above all for Sally who probably had no idea what she was doing. She had never cared before about the other woman. Charles took what he wanted. He did it cleanly and well, she thought, with a kind of admiration. He cut out remorse, carried himself with an athletic balance like a swimmer in a strong tide. She had never been foolish enough to stand in his way, knowing always that the tide would eventually turn back to her and quite willing to accept a double standard. But now it was different; she was responsible; she was involved in two ways.

Violet dreamed that she was caught in weeds at the bottom of a pond, waking half strangled by the sheet, in a sweat of fear. All night the rain and wind poured down against the windows.

Violet woke to the knowledge that she would have to intervene, warn. This was so against her nature that she forced herself quickly to get up, still in a dressing gown, before she might weaken in her resolution of the night, and climb the narrow stairs to speak to Sally.

"I have to go to the village," she said briskly, finding Sally smoking in bed, dropping ash into her saucer. "Why don't you come too? It's not a long walk and it will do us both good to get out into the air."

"Alone?" Sally asked, with so much hope flowing into her face that Violet winced.

"Of course, darling."

Sally felt wildly elated as they set out. She even loved the rain as they sloshed along, loved the feel of the big splashes of mud on her bare legs and the amazingly warm wet wind on her face.

"It's so warm," she said smelling the air. "Why haven't we done this before?"

Charles was disgruntled at being left behind, but Violet had been superb. She had said, "No Charles, we want to go alone. This is a female expedition."

Every now and then a gust of wind let fall a heavy shower from the trees overhead. Then they ducked and ran. They were quite breathless when they closed the gate and came out onto the main road, the dip and curve of it like a river, Sally thought, only a river that climbs hills. Walking beside Violet all her responses were heightened. There was no need to talk. Since two days before it seemed to Sally that communion had been established, not on her terms perhaps, but on Aunt Violet's, and as a result of this her eyes and every sense were awake, alive. She would have liked to lay her cheek against the wet grass and breathe in the smell of earth. The rain which touched her more actually even than sunlight seemed like a caress. The whole world had become a receptacle for the reverberations of love. She was very happy.

Now there came a lull in the wind, Violet decided that the moment had come to speak.

"Charles," she said, "is in one of his moods, I'm afraid."

"He's bored by the rain," Sally said quickly comforting for she caught the anxiety in Violet's tone, "but last night he seemed quite gay. Surely you're not worried, Aunt Violet?"

"Yes—no . . ." Violet walked on fast as if she could leave behind her what she had to say and didn't want to say. "Sally," she plunged in, because now they would be in the village in a few minutes, "you're a very attractive girl."

"But?" Sally was frozen with fear. She sensed that her aunt was going to say something withering. The tone was severe.

"But nothing. That's all." Violet had been walking too fast and was out of breath. She felt disgustingly tired.

"Why are you worried about Charles? Does he go into tailspins?" Sally couldn't believe it. Charles seemed so solid.

"In a way," Violet smiled at Sally's passionate directness. "This time it would not be a good idea. I thought I'd better warn you."

Sally absorbed this entirely unexpected statement slowly. It was true that Charles had been rather excited, true that he had, she supposed, flirted with her last night. But it was unbelievable that Violet should make an issue of this. It had meant nothing to her beyond a happy feeling of being admired and accepted. Was her aunt jealous of such a little thing?

"But Aunt Violet . . ." She said miserably, and then could go no further into a statement, nor for that matter along the road. They stood in the rain, Sally searching her aunt's face, but her aunt refused to lift her eyes. Violet was adjusting her raincoat nervously. She seemed absent.

"Sally, please understand," she said then, as sharply as if she were a governess. "These things happen. I have never minded."

"Why not?" Sally asked. "I should mind—dreadfully."

"Didn't you say something once about Ian and his women, his needing to be admired?"

"Ian's not my husband," said Sally shortly. In one second of violent revulsion she realized that she had really all the time been in love not only with Violet but with her marriage, with Charles and Violet as an entity. It was as if the atmosphere she had felt so powerfully, the thing she had resisted at first, the charm of these two people, the charm of their life together against which her relation with Ian was slowly disintegrating— as if all this now were breaking to pieces inside her. It was awful. What was left then? Life itself had become in a second cheap, sordid, not worth for a moment what it cost. Sally laughed a hard little laugh. She had never heard herself make such a sound before.

"Let's go," she said, "I want to see the village."

Violet was appalled at what she had done. She could at this moment have wept all the tears she had never wept through all the years of her marriage. In one way or another the innocence in her keeping had been damaged. And she was responsible.

"It might have been different if we'd had children," she said, trying to be reasonable, not to be sucked down into Sally's violent mood.

"No, it wouldn't have been different. Men are pigs, that's all. I might have known." Sally felt real horror that she had allowed Charles to touch her. What had he told Violet?

"Darling, please don't be so upset. Nothing will happen. It's all to be just the same, that's why I spoke at all, to keep it this way. Lately I've hoped, perhaps wrongly, that you were beginning to be happy here—"

"I wasn't happy," Sally said in her new hard voice. "But I was alive." She sounded as if life were now over and Violet restrained the smile which this violence compelled.

"I expect I've been talking nonsense—these days have got on our nerves. Will you forgive me?" They were approaching the first grey stone houses of the village, the slate roofs almost black in the rain. Violet felt panic rising in her.

"One doesn't forgive the truth," Sally said. "It's not a crime." She had turned away and was walking along ahead, not looking back.

It had been hard for Violet to speak at all. It had been a violation of her deep will not to discuss Charles. Now she was completely silenced. She followed Sally, caught up with her, and talked of other things. She did not know what she had done, nor why Sally seemed so angry and upset. Sally herself hardly knew.

It was a relief to them both when they came to the wine merchant's shop. Mrs. O'Connell, a woman with a kind plain face, greeted Violet warmly.

"Well, Mrs. Gordon. It's a pleasure to see you out on a day like this. Come in, come in, you'd better have a cup of tea."

"This is my American niece, Mrs. O'Connell, Sally Calvert."

"Your sister's daughter, is she? Well, Miss, I surely am glad to see you," she said, shaking hands and looking at Sally with a beaming smile. "You don't look like your mother, though," she added, "more like her great-grannie, isn't she?" she asked Aunt Violet. "She has her great-grannie's dark eyes."

She had led the way out of the rather dark shop into a small back parlor, with linoleum on the floor, three uncomfortable straight chairs in it, a vase with artificial flowers on the window sill, and two rather garish lithographs of the Holy Family. Sally looked around her with interest. Also she wanted to hear more about her great-grannie. She felt now that she must step behind

Aunt Violet and Uncle Charles, further back into the past, to find some safety.

"Tell me about my great-grannie, Mrs. O'Connell," Sally asked shyly when they had sat down in the three chairs.

"Oh your great-grannie was a love," Mrs. O'Connell said, getting up again. "Now Mrs. Gordon, may I offer you a glass of sherry—since you've brought your niece, and since it's such a wet morning?"

"Don't trouble," Violet said, but this Sally knew was one of the forms. Mrs. O'Connell came back with three glasses and a bottle. "It's the dry you like," she said.

"Well you're spoiling us . . ." Violet smiled her lovely smile, her famous smile. "Now tell us about Tommy. Has he passed the examination?"

"Next week, Mrs. Gordon. He's terribly nervous, you know. I can't do anything with him at all."

"Tommy is up for a scholarship at the University," Violet explained. "He's going to be a doctor, isn't he, Mrs. O'Connell?"

"So he says," Mrs. O'Connell beamed again. "I'm sure I don't know where he gets it from. I never could do a sum myself, and his father was a dunce, God rest his soul, though the kindest man who ever lived."

"Well here's to Tommy," Violet raised her glass.

"And how's Mr. Gordon?" Mrs. O'Connell asked. "And how does your niece find it here. It's your first visit, is it, Miss?" It was extraordinary Sally thought, what an atmosphere of friendship, of real interest and curiosity of the kindest nature flowed out from Mrs.

O'Connell's plain face. It was just the opposite of the gaucheness of the Desmonds, who from gaucheness perhaps, seemed to have no curiosity at all. They had not asked her even how she "found it here."

"I've never been in Ireland before. But I think it's lovely," she said, suddenly glad to be here in the little back parlor where so many things were taken for granted. Her aunt, for instance. Mrs. O'Connell was not a shop-keeper from whom one bought liquor, she was a friend. And her aunt was not the lady of the Great House but one of the Denes who had always been here, who were part of everything like the trees and the hills. It was very restful.

"She really hates the house," Aunt Violet said wickedly. But she couldn't resist.

"Oh no, Mrs. Gordon, you're teasing the poor child. Why her great-grannie used to say, every summer, she said it, right here in this very room, 'If I can just manage to die here in Dene's Court, Mrs. O'Connell, that's all I ask now.'"

"Did she die here?" Sally asked.

"No, the poor soul. She did not. She was taken in London, far from us all." Mrs. O'Connell thought about this with real feeling. Then, just as the skies did when the sudden bursts of sun broke through the massed clouds, she chuckled, "You may hate the old house," she said, looking mischievously at Sally, "but you'll come back, won't she, Mrs. Gordon? The Denes all come back to the house, sooner or later. Now who would have thought you and Mr. Gordon would be coming after all, you so far away, and the strange stamps on the Christmas cards? Many's the time I used to say to my husband, 'We'll never see Miss Violet,' and indeed he did not," she sighed. "But here you are. And a good thing it is too. We don't like to see the house empty." Then she asked again, "And how's Mr. Gordon?"

"At the moment I think he's cursing the weather," Violet said. "And we really must get back and cheer him up." She rose. They said good-bye and thank you. They waved at Mrs. O'Connell standing in the door.

"What a terribly nice woman," Sally said.

They felt warmer and the black mood had passed, thanks to Mrs. O'Connell. They could afford to walk quickly without speaking, without thinking. As she turned to fasten the gate behind them at the entrance to the long avenue, Sally realized that it was the second time she was coming back to the house. And even this brief excursion into the village, sad-looking, all dark grey stone, low houses one beside another, the post office that looked like a jail, an ugly brick church—even this hour away made a difference.

"We're nearly home," she said. Home? She had said "home." She had said it quite naturally, without thinking. It was strange.

Now they were coming round the bend from under the dripping trees, they saw the house from the side, buttressed at the back by the offices and stables, and from here, somewhat softened and sheltered by the high trees. It had stopped raining. There was only the sound of dripping from the leaves, from the gutters and a seeping

159

crepitant sound of earth absorbing water, and the sound of their own steps loudly crunching the gravel.

Charles came out on the terrace, looked up at the sky, and waved a welcome to them and to the clearing weather. For a second the scene appeared to Sally like an engraving "The Return." We have been on a long journey, she thought, and now we are coming home. But then she remembered (and it disgusted her like the sight of a large fat slug on the path) what Aunt Violet had said about Charles, about the marriage. All of this is false then, all of it, she thought, except—and she looked up at the steadying, implacable stone face of the house—except You. You, she thought, are real, steadfast, pure, all that we are not.

She walked up to the terrace alone and went in, hardly glancing at Charles. What she wanted was to find the portrait of her great-grandmother on the wall.

Then as if it was the only possible thing to do she went straight down the back stairs to the kitchen. Sally stood in the doorway and looked around for a moment before she was noticed. Annie was back to her at the stove pouring hot water onto tea. Maire was sitting at the table, polishing silver and so intent that she did not lift her head. It had the homeliness and beauty of a scene painted by one of the Flemish painters where the humblest occupations and objects are quietly exalted. Sally looked with amazement at the huge tureens and spiders hanging by the stove, at the shelves still filled with the oil lamps and candles of other days, and felt the peace, the continuity of all this, of the innumerable cups of tea that had been sipped here, and the innumerable fires lit while upstairs personal relations wound and unwound themselves, feverish and unreal.

"Hello," she said, "may I have a cup of tea?"

"Surely, Miss, and welcome," Annie beamed upon her.

"I wondered how long it would take you to find your way down. I've been expecting you," she said, laying out the cups and saucers, as Maire pushed aside her cloth and looked shyly at Sally.

"What a wonderful kitchen!" Sally said.

Annie laughed, "Wonderful it may be, but it's dark and gloomy, and that's a fact."

"I like it," Sally said, going over to the stove and warming her hands.

"And so did your mother," Annie said nodding her approval. "Your mother used to spend hours down here, baking her dolls' food, you know, and crying in Annie's lap too, the poor little thing."

"Why was she poor?" Sally asked, sitting down at the table and holding up her cup for Annie to pour into. She looked hard at Annie's face which she had not really seen before. It gave one a feeling of security. It must have always looked exactly as it did now, except that the straggly topknot was flecked with white.

"Sure, it's a long story and I'll not be boring you with it." This was clearly a prelude. Sally stirred her tea, adding more milk. It tasted wonderfully better than the tea upstairs.

"I guess she minded Aunt Violet," Sally said, to lead Annie on, for she could guess what was coming.

"Mind is not the word. She suffered cruelly. And there was nothing Miss Violet could do about it, kind as she is and was. But she couldn't have done more harm if she'd laid a curse, and that's a fact," Annie said, shaking her head. "So it was right and fair that your mother went faraway over the ocean to find her happiness, sad as it was to see her leave the house and not return."

"Why is it a curse to be so beautiful? Why isn't it a blessing?" Sally asked. "Hasn't Aunt Violet herself been happy?" she asked, for she felt Annie knew everything she wanted to find out and would tell her now.

Annie stirred her tea and drank two sips loudly. "No children," she said, "for one thing."

"But that isn't because she's beautiful—is it?—I mean . . ." Sally glanced over at Maire and felt shy. She wondered what Maire was thinking. It was nice for once to be sitting at table with her, she seemed so much less shy here.

"Well, there are women meant to bear children—your mother was one—and women not meant to," Annie said mysteriously. "It's all a mystery, but the trouble for your Aunt Violet was that she was the cause of misery, and yet could do nothing about it."

"Did she use to come down and cry too?" Sally asked mischievously.

"That she did," Annie said with satisfaction. "That she did."

"It's nice they've come back, isn't it?" Sally said warmly.

"It's the will of God," Annie said solemnly and Maire nodded her head in solemn agreement. "The Denes come back to the old house. However far they go and how long they stay, they always come back. For the house is the blood in their veins and without it they wither away."

"Mother hasn't withered away," Sally said, withdrawing instinctively from this old wives' tale, and from the tone.

"No," Annie said, not at all put out by the blunt statement, "she had to go over the ocean to find her way, and there's always a Dene that does that, just as there's always a Dene to come back."

"I wonder which I am," Sally said thoughtfully. It had never entered her head that she might be drawn into some inevitable current, some tide of the past, that coming here was like a fate and not just a punishment. "You know I was sent here to get me away from Ian, the boy

163

I'm going to marry. He's an actor," she said simply, wondering what Annie's reaction would be.

"An actor, is he?" Annie said, her eyes lighting up with surprise or delight. "Miss Violet never told me he was an actor," she said as if this were a serious omission, and she had not been quite given her due. "And does he make a living at it, if I may ask?"

"Well"—Sally thought this over—"I don't know really. You see, he has money of his own. He's quite rich, as a matter of fact, not that it matters."

"Well, if he's so rich and can do as he pleases, then what's the harm?" Annie said practically. "And handsome he must be if he's an actor."

"He's beautiful," Sally said, but even as she said it, she felt a qualm. It was a long time since she had really felt him as a presence. If she said beautiful, she thought of Aunt Violet, not of Ian. "But oh Annie, he's so far away, I feel I'm beginning to forget him. It's awful," she said passionately.

"Well, it won't be forever, doatie, you'll go back and find him if he's your true love."

True love, Sally said the words over to herself. What did they mean? They sounded like some old poem, not quite real, or was it that Ian was no longer quite real? She looked around the kitchen again as if to test something against it, or find something. And she remembered what Aunt Violet had said about her uncle.

"I don't believe there is such a thing, Annie," she said bitterly. "People are just beasts."

Annie who had no way of knowing about what Sally was thinking was taken aback.

"Yes," Maire said to everyone's surprise, "that's what I think, Miss. That's just what I think."

"You don't think at all," Annie said contemptuously.

But Maire was looking at Sally with wide-open intense eyes as if she had at long last met someone who knew what life was all about.

"Even Aunt Violet and Uncle Charles aren't true loves, not really," she said quietly.

"They're not perfect," Annie said crossly, "who would wish them to be? Two such beautiful people, surely that's enough—and what more would you be asking for, Miss Sally, if I may be so bold?"

"Nothing, Annie—only . . ."

"Life's a cruel business, full of shame and temptation," Annie said, shaking her head, "but you and Maire are too young still and you want what cannot be, and so you'll be suffering," she said with a sudden warm smile, "my poor doaties." In this kitchen Sally realized suddenly everything was a drama and so everything was bearable, because usually one felt one was exaggerating and being foolish, but Annie would meet one halfway, glorying in approaching disaster like a general in an approaching battle. It was very restful.

Sally came up from the dark kitchen stairs into the house, empty, still, and flooded with sunlight. Charles and Violet had gone out of course; Violet would be in the walled garden examining the ruins of the roses with Cammaert. With something like relief, with a tremor of fear, Sally thought, I'm all alone here. She stood on the threshold of the library as if waiting for some decision which would take her inside, to her grandfather's desk. Far-off on the hill a sheep coughed.

The house now seemed the exact concrete equivalent of her state of mind. She felt empty, tired but also flooded with peace. For a few moments more she could stand like this, suspended outside of life, and catch her breath. In the last hours a whole part of herself had crumbled away, innocence, childhood, she imagined, like a shell, and she was standing grown-up, but completely exposed. The loneliness was acute, but also exhilarating. She knew she was free, free of the terrible hunger which had bound her to Violet and to Charles. She saw now that their life was not her life, and her wish to crash through into it by force of love was only an evasion of her own life, the desire to take something already created, to hide from reality in a world of imagination where everything could be heightened because untrue. Her feeling about Violet and Charles would become true perhaps if she could come to look at them without wishing either to possess or to be possessed by what they had. I have got to know where I stand, Sally thought, making her decision. She felt backed up by Annie's sense of drama, by the ease with which Annie confronted, at least in conversation, impossible situations. Somewhere across this loneliness, across this sunlight, this emptiness which was already invaded by his presence, was Ian. Sally crossed the library as if she were crossing an ocean, went to the desk and took a sheet of paper out of the top drawer. When Violet came in an hour later, she was sealing the envelope.

"Sally darling, what are you doing indoors? It's too lovely out—"

"I've been thinking," Sally said, laying the letter down on the desk and turning in her chair to face her aunt, with an absence of personal emotion which almost frightened her. Standing in the doorway, tentative, kind, her aunt seemed diminished and Sally, standing felt immensely tall and strong; so much so that she shrank before the shock she was about to administer. She had not until this second thought of her decision in terms of

Violet. So she spoke quickly, to get it over. "Ian wants to fly over for the weekend. I've just written to tell him to come."

"Come here?" Violet looked at the letter on the desk as if it were a bomb. Then she sat down, rather slowly, to give herself time. Sally saw the flush of anger or dismay creeping up her throat. "But Sally dear," she said in the reasonable voice of someone determined to be controlled, "I think you should have asked me first."

"I know. Please don't be cross," Sally warded off what she felt was sure to come. "It's just that it all has become impossible. After our walk, I mean. I feel now that I must be sure about Ian. I have to know." Saying this aloud, Sally felt doubts and fears all around her waiting to pounce.

"But how *can* he come? Fly the Atlantic for a weekend?" This was a world of which Violet knew nothing, this American world where people moved about with frightening rapidity, where journeys which normal people would plan for a year were undertaken at a moment's whim.

"Oh, he has plenty of money, and very little time," Sally answered, on the defensive now too. "It would only be for a few days, after all."

"But, Sally," Violet said coldly, for she was beginning to realize all the implications. Sally's tone was quite implacably sure of itself. "Your mother sent you here just so that you would not see Ian for a time. How can I have him as a guest in this house? Don't you see?"

Violet's icy reasonableness had its effect. Sally's new-found maturity and self-reliance wavered before it. She was terrified of losing Violet's regard, imagined with intense clarity what suffering it would mean to be shut out now by Violet. Searching Violet's clear blue gaze and abashed before it, the words were flung out like anger, only they were love. "It's just that I need to have him, so I'll know something. Oh, I feel so confused and empty—" She commanded herself to stay calm, not to cry. "I'm upset," she said. "Can't you understand? Charles—"

"I was terribly wrong to say what I did," Violet answered in the same cold dry voice. She was so angry, so inexplicably angry that she could have gladly shaken Sally.

And this anger reached Sally like a blow. "No—no . . ." she murmured and ran to where her aunt was sitting, and knelt by the chair. "Only don't you see? I'm nothing. I'm lost. I've got to try to be myself. It's all been too much, these last days, the rain, everything pressing down. I've felt so queer, you don't know." Sally fought for words and then gave up. "It was the best I could do," and finding the way that was not words now, she lifted Violet's hand and pressed it to her breast in a gesture so intense that Violet felt tears rising in her own eyes. "I think," Sally added, "that I have been a little in love with you."

Then she ran from the room.

Violet went to the sideboard and poured herself a drink. All their lives she and Barbie had avoided ever coming to the point of antagonism and realized love that she and Sally had just passed. Violet was humbled by it, humbled and in some way armed. She had made her decision. If Ian came, she would not tell her sister. She knew now that her first loyalty was not to Barbie, not even to Charles, but to Sally because such innocence calls out our first loyalty and in its presence there can be no other.

Charles, unaware of anything that had happened, was full of well-being now that the sun had come out. He had plans to take Sally with him to see the farm, to drive up among the hills; he preferred to think of this as a journey with her alone. After all, Violet hated to be wrenched out of her habits and customs and really liked being in the house and garden better than moving about. Charles whistled happily as he strode about in one of the far plantations, marking trees to be cut. He did not think further than this plan to take Sally out. Nothing, in his own mind, could have been more innocent. It was a useful good idea to get her mind off that bounder, in any case. A minor flirtation would be the best thing in the world for Sally. She was a queer little thing, Charles thought, for he was not going to admit how powerfully attractive she had become in the last few days, and she seemed to be avoiding him. Probably more went on in her dark head than anyone knew. Possibly she was more attracted to him than she herself could admit. This idea startled Charles. He snapped the knife shut with which he had been marking trees and held it tightly in one hand. Then he told himself severely that he was an old fool. Then he laughed out loud and stamped noisily out of the underbrush and down the hill to the house. He felt younger than he had for a year, in a mood for practical jokes, for teasing Violet who hated above all be to teased. Life, he said to himself, is good.

He said it again aloud to Violet when he finally found her picking sweet peas in the walled garden. He stood just behind her and told her that life was good.

"Yes, dear," Violet said patiently.

"Don't be so priggish, Violet—it's good, I tell you."

"I'm not priggish, I'm just agreeing with you. What's priggish about that?"

Violet was evidently in one of her perverse moods. She was paying great attention to each flower, rearranging the bunch in her hands, and not looking at him. Charles picked a bright pink sweet pea, came round behind her and tickled her neck with the crisp teasing flower.

"Darling, must you? I really want to get this done."

"You and Queen Victoria," he muttered darkly and

then he laughed such a gay and simple laugh that Violet found herself laughing too. "You're a perfect wretch, Charles."

"You see," he said in triumph, "you are amused. You can't help being amused, because it's such a lovely day. Let's have a drink before lunch and sit out as if we were the rich and idle, on the terrace . . ."

Violet, hemmed in by two dangerous kinds of innocence, felt beaten. Why not enjoy the day and all that it held? Why worry and be responsible? After all, if Ian did come it might solve everything. She pressed her nose into the cool perfumed faces of the sweet peas.

"How can we be so old and beautiful?" Charles was saying in his caressing happy voice.

"How can we be so old?" Violet echoed, laughing at him now. "You are a very old frisky lamb, darling," she said, taking his arm and turning down the path towards the creaking gate in the wall.

"A ram—a ram—a ram—" he said loudly. "But really, Violet, look at the wall. It's in a terrible way, isn't it? And I must do something about the gate."

"Does it feel like a real life, Charles?" Violet turned to him gravely, as they closed the gate behind them.

"You sound like Sally."

"She keeps asking what it all means, doesn't she? I begin to ask myself . . ." In the shadow of the wall after the brilliant sunlight, it felt cold. She would have liked to lean her head on Charles's shoulder, to be supported and enclosed and cherished. But she saw another light altogether in his eyes and saw that he was not at that second thinking of her at all, though he was looking straight at her.

"Of course it's a real life," he said briskly. "Come along. Let's find the child and have a drink."

"Sally thinks we're useless, battening on the poor," Violet said, grasping at an argument as one way of getting Charles's attention.

"That's what college does to women, fills their heads up with half-baked notions, sociology, what? Economics, what? She'd learn more by living on a farm for a year. I really must do something about the nettles," he interrupted himself as they passed the neglected stables. "One of these days I'm going to take Sally around, give her a few lessons in practical economics right here."

"Yes, dear," Violet said patiently. But this time he let her tone pass in silence. He was running ahead, up the steps of the terrace, and Violet stopped to watch him, and found that she minded a good deal his blaze of energy, his unconsciousness, his self-enclosure. Sometimes she looked forward to their old age, to the peace of it. We'll read she thought. The danger will be past. But she could not really imagine such a time, nor really wish for it. The house, she thought, looking up at it, is a challenge. It was not built in a safe time for safety, nor for any kind of peaceful dying. It was built to maintain, to endure, built in danger and on belief. Thinking of it thus, she felt an old courage in her. She felt armed.

"Where have you been?" Sally asked, finding them settled in deck chairs. "I looked all over. I've got news," she said, carefully unfolding a cablegram. "Ian's flying over for a few days next Friday—he's really coming. I can't believe it. Oh Aunt Violet, I'm scared," she said, curling up suddenly at Violet's feet, hugging her knees.

"What's this?" Charles asked so angrily that Violet looked up and tried to warn him with a glance.

"Ian's coming. Do you mind?" Sally said coldly.

"I don't understand. Did you invite him, Violet?" Charles was standing now, glaring down at them like some god disturbed in his lair, Violet thought.

"Not exactly," she said, laying a hand on Sally's head as if to reassure her before the storm, for it was to be a storm. Charles had been taken by surprise, a thing he hated above all, and he had been left out, a thing he resented. "Sally told me she had asked him to fly over and by then it seemed too late to refuse."

"And does Sally's mother know this?" Charles asked.

"I'm not going to tell Barbie," Violet said, looking him straight in the eye.

"Violet, I presume you consider this my house as well as yours?"

"Of course."

"Why didn't you at least ask me, then?" Charles didn't know why he was so angry, but he knew that anger had taken possession of him like a temporary illness. Obscure humiliations out of the past, the fact that Violet's family was a distinguished one in a sense that his had never been, that this was her estate and that the people on it looked to her rather than to him, her way of treating him sometimes as if he were a child, all these buried angers focused now on this given situation and burned inside him.

"I suppose I didn't tell you because of the way you are behaving now. I thought Ian might not come and there was no point in making an issue of it. I'm sorry, Charles"—she shrugged her shoulders, a gesture which negated the apology—"I should have told you, of course."

Sally felt as if she had been transported into the middle of a storm. Because she was sitting on the step, close to Aunt Violet's knees, and Charles was standing over them, both he and her aunt loomed very large and quite terrifying. This fierce grating of their natures hurt her as a dog is hurt by music and she would have liked, like a dog, to howl. She didn't at the moment care at all whether Ian came or not, but only that this frightfully painful scene should stop. If only, she thought, I could just vanish. But there she was between them, with no escape possible, short of making a scene herself.

"You are always taking decisions out of my hands, Violet, and in this case it's inexcusable. I suppose we can cable and tell him not to come? You may feel you can do this behind your sister's back but I cannot. After all, she trusts us."

If they had been alone, Violet would have had an answer to that; she bit her lip. Instead she turned and deliberately looked out at the grove of oak trees as if she could project herself into its cool shade in a single concentrated look.

"Violet, I asked you a question. Can we cable and put this madness off?"

"I'll tell mother myself," Sally said then.

"You'll do nothing of the sort. This is my responsibility," Violet answered quickly. "Charles," she tried to smile, "please be reasonable. He'll only be here a week-end."

"After all," Sally said for she was getting angry now too, "I'm engaged to the man."

"You're nothing but a child."

"I'm twenty-one." She glared at Charles who glared back.

"You're both children," Violet announced and laughed her slightly theatrical laugh. But it had been the wrong moment to choose to break Charles's rising fury of impotence.

"Damn it, Violet, I'm not a child and I'm sick and tired of being treated as one. Will you listen to me!" he roared, quite red in the face. Sally instinctively withdrew farther along the step. He looked as if he would become violent at any moment.

"Yes, dear," Violet said in her patient voice.

"And don't put me off with that priggish smug tone of voice. All my life I've had to listen to that tone of voice—"

"Poor Charles," Violet said ironically. "You have had a hard life." She knew very well that all he wanted was to make her really angry. Then the whole thing would blow up and blow over, but Violet would not give in this time. And there was Sally who evidently minded this very much and did not understand it and would not forgive. It must not turn into a serious argument, at all costs.

Abruptly Charles sat down. He felt sore from top to bottom, sore and at cross-purposes with himself and with everyone else. It was humiliating beyond words that Sally should witness his defeat. All his joy in himself, in the morning, in the goodness of life had withered away and Charles felt old and diminished.

Both he and Violet were too absorbed in themselves to notice that Sally was crying. But once the tears began she could not stop them and now she gave a little sobbing croak.

"What is the matter, Sally?" Charles said crossly. He felt ashamed. "Now look what you've done, Violet."

"What *I've* done!" Violet was suddenly furious. "You talk about responsibility, Charles, but you can't take it."

"Oh please—please—please don't." Sally, sobbing, got up. "It's all my fault," she said in a desperate attempt to appease the jealous gods. "Only . . ." and she broke down completely, and ran down the terrace steps and off down the road, where she did not know. All she wished was to get away from them, from the house, from all that was happening so much beyond her control, so deeply disturbing.

"Let her go, Charles," Violet said harshly, as Charles moved to follow. "Don't you dare follow her."

She was standing now too. They faced each other. For a second all they could feel was the immense vacuum Sally left behind her. The letdown was as great as the tension had been. They were actors alone on a stage before an empty house. It was Violet, with her quick honest perception who knew this and so was the first to drop into her chair with a sigh and pick up her drink. Then she said in a normal tone of voice, quite quietly and as if she had complete confidence in Charles, and all the words they had spoken were just a scene they had played out, but now they had become real people again and left the play,

"This is all about Sally, really, isn't it, Charles?"

Charles looked down at her quizzically, humbly, tenderly, and said, "The maddening thing about you, Violet, is that you always know these things about half a second before I do, so you always win."

"Dear," she said then and it was her turn to look a little ashamed of herself, "don't you see, that's why I thought it quite clever of me to let Ian come?"

"But Violet," he protested, "I never meant—"

"Of course, darling, but she is very attractive—and vulnerable—and innocent—and so, darling, are you."

Charles resisted her smile, but he was ready to capitulate. "I hate the idea of this actor, this—this—self-satisfied success-boy who can fly about as if it were nothing at all. A weekend indeed!"

"I don't think it's such a foolish idea either to let Sally see him in these particular surroundings." Violet added, "I'm hoping he won't altogether fit in."

But Charles was not listening. He had had a shock. He was beginning to see what the summer madness had almost led him into and felt shaken. It was hard, feeling guilty as he did, to forgive Violet for her prescience. He could not quite forgive her, as a matter of fact.

"We are getting old, Violet. It's disgusting to get old," he said out of all this.

"If you fight it with the wrong weapons, it may be disgusting," Violet said tentatively.

"Whatever are you talking about?" Charles bristled.

It was not the moment to try to talk this over and Violet knew it. "Never mind, darling, you said yourself a half-hour ago that we are old and beautiful—remember?"

"I was boasting," Charles said cruelly.

"I expect you were, darling," Violet said, lifting a hand to her face as if to shield it. "I think the truth is that we're both rather spoiled, far more spoiled than Sally, for instance. We have rather a lot to learn, Charles, you know . . ." but this Charles was not ready to concede, not yet.

Still, the scene on the terrace had sobered them. They had come out, each in his own way, chastened, relieved to find each other sane and simple as after a storm. The

179

next days seemed suspended at the meridian of summer. Never again would the sun be so hot, the grass so sweet-smelling, the trees so fresh and lush, nor the twilights so beautifully long. "Still pond, no more moving," Sally thought. And indeed they seemed at times like players in a game of Blind Man's Buff, waiting to be touched by Ian, the only possible It. The intimate music Sally had captured, as she leaned out of the window and looked down at Aunt Violet and Uncle Charles standing in the path, now included her. They were for the first time, able to be silent together—Aunt Violet looking like an angel in a niche in an old basket-chair Charles had found in the cellar; Charles, relaxed after a morning of tramping about, a glass in his hand, occasionally making a remark which no one answered; Sally lying flat on her back on some cushions, looking up dreamily at the darkening sky, at the small motion of the leaves as they stirred just before darkness fell, and the stones of the house warmed in the afterglow. At such times she wished that they could go on a little while just as they were. I shall never be the same again, she thought. What disturbing violent sweetness would Ian bring with him, forcing her back where decisions had to be made, where she must meet huge unknown forces in herself, in him? Sally was afraid. She had been afraid ever since her decision. Almost, she wished she had not made it.

She saw the episode of her attachment to Violet as an episode, a clarification, the revenge of life itself perhaps on her deliberate shutting out and refusal of all

180

experience here, on her having called it and willed it to be a prison. Yet it had changed her. She felt much older and in some ways, more vulnerable. She had had a glimpse of what passion could be. And she wondered how she would meet Ian—would he be the same? Would he blot out everything and take her back with one triumphant kiss? Was he coming because he had at last decided to ask her to marry him? This thought brought Sally to her feet; she stretched and lifted her arms to the sky in a gesture of hope and abandon. Then she sat down again, with a long sigh—the suspense of these days!

Never again, Violet thought, moved by the unconscious wordless hope in Sally's look and stretch towards the sky; never again would the curve of the hill as it rose and encircled the house seem as gentle, nor the long gold rays of the sun lie across the fields with such extreme beauty. It was the still moment before a major change. From her basket-chair she looked over at Charles (who was still rather distant for he hadn't quite forgiven her) and thought they had reached a plateau in their marriage. Later they would take life up again, and they would find out how they had changed, but for the moment it was a rest to have no emotional demands made upon her, to sit here quietly and sew with a sense of being both very completely herself and also, in some way, all the women who had sat on this terrace in the late summer evenings.

In this mood she turned to Sally and said, "It was a

wonderful thing when your father came here, so many years ago. It was wonderful to see Barbie grow up overnight."

"Why did he come?" Sally sat up, hugging her knees, while the rooks suddenly rose in the air, then settled again like a noisy sigh in the trees.

"It was an accident really. He was staying with friends and wanted to see the house. So they drove over. He was such a silent guest, I hardly noticed him at first —the house was full up and I had two jealous young men to cope with myself—but Barbie liked him plainly, and soon she got him laughing. You know how funny she can be when she's in the mood . . ." Sally nodded solemnly. This was her mother, but it was also in a queer way herself she was hearing about. When Ian came would she too grow up in a night?

"It was extraordinary because Barbie had never liked anyone since her unhappy experience with Philip. She just refused to be interested, so it seemed like a miracle, happening so suddenly—I'll never forget how she came to my room that night (we had hardly communicated for months) and flung herself down on the bed, kicking off her shoes and said, 'Oh Violet, will he come back? He's such a peculiar creature . . .' "

Violet talked on, borne on the current of happy memories, as if at long last she had come to the point in her journey into the past when she could rest on the happy memories, when she could accept the whole and not be torn apart any longer by the broken parts.

The brilliant last rays of the sun were suddenly gone, and the stone terrace felt cold. And then Violet looked up and saw the tension in Sally's face, the eyes so wide-open as if she was looking with a sort of cold triumph at the future. What was she thinking of? Her father had been so keen, so distinguished and calm—could Ian meet this figure and stand up against it?

But Sally was thinking with a wave of pride in the past, of almost arrogance, that she and the house waited alone for Ian, who could not possibly imagine what majesty of youth and age, and what judgment would stand on the terrace to greet him, she with the house behind her and its great cold eyes staring out behind hers. This was the image she created to protect herself against her rising fears, her rising weakness and love. For the first time, she thought, I have something. I'm protected.

The Friday they had waited for so happily and in such suspense threw them back roughly into time, into getting up at four o'clock in the morning, Sally's teeth actually chattering in the cold, and Charles still half-asleep, growling and cross.

"Drive carefully, Charles, and be sure to see that Sally eats a good breakfast in Shannon. You'll have plenty of time . . ."

Sally managed a wan smile when she was in the car. She felt rather sick.

Violet went back to bed, crept between the cold sheets, wide awake, and smoked a cigarette. For the last time she reckoned up as the grey dawn came what it would cost not to have told Barbie and for the last time decided that she would stand by her decision, and take the consequences. Perhaps later, after Ian had come and gone, she could explain the matter. But what if he was coming to make a definite proposal? Somehow she doubted that and felt that Sally, who had undoubtedly thought of it, doubted it too. Why then? To break the whole thing off? He didn't sound as if he cared enough about other people to take all that trouble. It was all too mysterious and queer, the very color of daylight so grim and pale, and the furniture looming up in the half-dark. Violet missed Charles. She found it quite impossible to go back to sleep. Everything was at sixes and sevens, she felt, and she resented the intruder. After all, they had made their peace. He was not necessary, for all Sally thought. Violet's nervousness increased as the morning finally came, a brilliant morning, with bold sunlight flooding the room.

At ten Violet was dressed and the dew had dried on

the grass. She stood on the terrace, peering down the drive, wondering why they did not come? Was the plane late?

It distracted her to think for a moment of all the arrivals this terrace had seen, and that there was no way to approach the house more simply, more discreetly. All arrivals had to be formal, had to come down the winding drive and climb the steps of the terrace and to see the house for the first time at its most formidable, standing straight up in the air, unsoftened by perspective. The house always won the first round, she thought, with satisfaction. And any arrival must feel at first slightly diminished in stature and slightly in awe, even if he did not show it (here she chuckled remembering) by falling down on the bottom step. Here Charles had ridden up, dismounted, and she remembered shaded his eyes and frowned as he examined the façade; here Barbie's young man had appeared, one among several faces in the carriage—and they had looked at the horses first and not at him; they had exclaimed at the beauty of the greys, perfectly matched, and never for a moment imagined that in the carriage was a young man who would take Barbie so far away and make her happy and produce Sally.

Violet was deep in these memories and enjoying them, when the whirr of the car became distinct. She ran down the steps as if suddenly she did not want to be formal nor formidable, as if her heart had intervened for Sally's sake, and she would mitigate the arrival in every way she could.

Whatever she had imagined, it was not at all the young man who came gravely towards her and bowed in a slightly foreign way as he shook her hand, and then smiled a dazzling smile as he said,

"This is such an adventure, Mrs. Gordon." It was his turn now to look up at the house, to frown slightly, and then to say to Charles with imperturbable self-assurance, "What perfect proportions!"

"Not bad, eh?" Charles said, and in the tone of his voice Violet read a greal deal. He did not like Ian, but he had not been able to be contemptuous of him. That was something.

Sally was standing at a little distance from them.

"Well, children," Violet said, trying to weld the disparate group into an entity, "we'd better come in. . . . Did you have a decent breakfast in Shannon?" she asked, slipping an arm through Sally's while Charles and Ian took the elegant leather bag out of the car and argued politely about who would carry it up.

They sat in the library where Violet had lit the fire though the day would be hot, and drank coffee. They had time now to look at each other. Ian, Violet noted, was dressed almost too impeccably in a grey tweed jacket, with a foulard round his neck, a yellow sweater, grey flannels and some sort of American moccasins made of suede. He did not seem quite real, though very much more presentable than she had foreseen. He was almost too sure of himself, too polite, leaping to his feet whenever she rose, lighting her cigarette very gracefully, and in general as slightly too impeccable as his clothes. But he had, she must grant, a handsome, even a distinguished face, good bones and a firm wide mouth to set off the very dark eyes and long lashes.

"You must be exhausted," Violet said, refilling his cup.

"Well, not exactly. But I would love to shave and have a wash."

"You can't have a bath," Sally said, "you know." She seemed rather pleased to forbid him something he might expect.

"Oh well," he laughed easily, "I'm clean under the surface, though you might not know it." In fact he looked too clean, Violet thought.

"What an adventure!" he said again, after he had looked around the room, taking it all in, Violet thought, as if it were a stage set, and then aware a little uncomfortably that he was taking her in too.

"Can you believe you were in New York last night?" Sally asked. There was always in her speech to him a directness, almost a blunt quality as if she must cut through to find him, as if she must protect herself by a manner where he was concerned. And she had chosen to be honest and direct where another girl might have chosen to be devious and flattering.

"No, I can't." Then he turned again to Violet, "Sally's looking superb, isn't she?" He said it, Violet thought, in a slightly patronizing way.

"I'm glad you think we've taken good care of her," Violet answered simply. "It has been lovely for us to have her here, hasn't it, Charles?"

"As foreign occupations go, it has been bearable," he granted. He had meant it as a humorous remark, but it turned out to have a barb in it and Sally felt it. He felt it too, and was sorry, and made matters worse by trying to mend things. "At first we were treated rather roughly, but lately we have been given a few privileges—"

"The barbarian is being gradually civilized, he means," Sally said quickly.

"What made you a barbarian at first?" Ian asked, with real interest. "What is it we do wrong?" He turned to Violet. "One's always hearing about it, the awful behavior of Americans. In what way?" he persisted in his gentle elaborately polite voice.

Sally giggled with pleasure at the remembrance. "Oh, I wore jeans to dinner and played jazz all morning, and didn't wear shoes you can wade through brooks in —what else, Uncle Charles? Oh yes, the worst—I fell downstairs the day I arrived—or rather upstairs, the terrace steps," she amended, suffused with laughter, "and Aunt Violet thought I was drunk."

They all laughed now except Ian, who seemed left out.

"Were you?" he asked. It was the first thing he had said or done that was out of key, that suggested New York, night clubs. . . .

"Of course not," Sally said briefly. And then as if she could not sustain the conversation a moment longer, as if she must while still on this wave of merriment manage to get him away to herself, she got up quickly, went over and pulled him up by one hand and said, "Come and meet Annie in the kitchen. She's dying to meet you." She gathered the cups onto the tray and took it, a thing she had never done before. "And then you can unpack," she added over her shoulder. Ian held the door for her to pass through and closed it carefully behind them.

"Well?" Violet asked Charles.

"Well?" Charles asked Violet.

"It's not quite what we expected, is it? Such a flawless young man," Violet said thoughtfully. She was puzzled.

"He's read up on Ireland all right," Charles chuckled, "asked me questions. Put on quite a show as a matter of fact."

"How is he with Sally?"

"How should I know? Sally sat in the back seat and hardly said a word."

"One doesn't *know*," Violet said teasing him, "one senses."

"My senses were rather busy driving and talking," Charles said, piqued.

What Violet's sense had been, she did not say. It was too soon. But she was slightly troubled. She had caught Ian's appraising, almost conspiratorial glance. And she had wondered just what it meant.

Alone in her room for a few minutes while Ian shaved across the ballroom in the opposite corner of the house, Sally lay down on the bed. She felt wildly nervous. She had forgotten what it was like to be with him, always with other people, always under the strain of trying to communicate *across* something—as if shouting in a high wind. That was why touch was so important and, she realized with dismay, he had hardly touched her except for that rather formal kiss at the airport. Of course he had been sitting in the front seat—but still —for days she had been wound up tight to this moment of his arrival as if it would inevitably be a moment of release. Now she realized that it was only the beginning of three days of even greater strain. How do people live all their lives among personal relations? she thought. How do they ever do it?

She bounced up and went to the window, looked at her watch, saw that this eternity of waiting had only been one minute and a half, and then looked out. At least, she reminded herself, her worst fears had not been realized. Uncle Charles had been darling with Ian and so had Aunt Violet and Ian himself was behaving beautifully—except (here Sally sat down again on the bed, her chin in her hands)—there was something wrong with the way he talked to Annie, in fact the visit to the kitchen had not been a success. Queer, because this had been the one thing of which she was not afraid—Annie would understand. Annie would know. But Annie had been treated so formally. Ian hadn't even shaken hands with her. He had been embarrassed, she felt, and after a few minutes she had rescued him by taking him upstairs. And now perhaps Annie's feelings had been hurt.

I shall never live through this, she thought. It is too complicated. She turned on the radio for the first time in ten days. There was a French crooner. Then she lay down on the bed again and just waited for Ian to come. Slowly, very slowly, she felt the vice of tension, which held her, loosen a little. It would be all right if he would just come in and kiss her a great deal and tell her that he loved her.

It was almost an hour later and she was still lying on her bed, entirely given over to sensation, her love prickling at the tips of her fingers and toes and up and down her spine, when the knock came.

"Come on out, Sally!"

"Oh come in," she said running to the door, and then

standing there on the sill, not moving, just waiting. "Oh Ian," she said from somewhere deep down inside her, in a new grave voice, a little husky.

But he didn't kiss her. "Glad to see me?" he asked, standing there, smiling into her eyes, as if she were one of any number of people, but not just herself.

Sally nodded. Then he walked in and looked around, went to the windows, looked down at the driveway curving out and up among the trees, and seemed for the moment to have forgotten her.

"Your aunt's quite devastating, isn't she?" His back was still turned.

Sally did not like the way he said this, the slightly ironical tone of his voice, as if her aunt were a curiosity like a Sheraton table to be examined dispassionately and granted a passing compliment by a connoisseur. She felt suddenly that her room had been invaded and changed. It was no longer the room where she had lain so warm and flowing a few moments before.

"I suppose she's what the English call 'a lovely,' isn't she?" Ian turned, quite unconscious apparently of what he was doing. Sally stayed in the doorway. "Every gesture is conscious, and that wonderful Edwardian laugh."

"Good God, Ian, you sound as if she were ninety."

Ian sat on the window sill, swinging his legs carelessly, looking down into the garden. "She might as well be. Her kind is pretty well extinct."

"You're being mean on purpose. Stop it," Sally commanded. Ian, amused by her vehemence, stopped swinging his leg and got up. "I'm fascinated, you silly. I'm absolutely fascinated," he assured her. "Can't make the uncle out," he added as if the only thing in the world that could possibly interest him was the Gordons.

"Uncle Charles is a very distinguished man," Sally said coldly.

"What does he do with himself all day?"

"He's trying to get the place on its feet—they've been away for years. He has to see to the estate, the farm, the woods, all that. He's very busy, as a matter of fact."

"Well, it's an amazing old place, I must say," Ian granted. "Pretty Chekhovian"—Sally winced remembering that she had once used this very word and with almost his contempt—"pretty dilapidated."

Sally looked quickly around the room as if to defend it, but she said nothing. With every word Ian said, he was receding. She was afraid of attacking him now. She sat down on the bed, but Ian was already on the move,

"I'd like to see it all—will you take me on a grand tour?"

She remembered now how often he irritated her and then with one sentence like this, some grace in his bearing, the caressing tone of his voice, all the irritation vanished. She had never known why she loved him (she often found him unbearable) but she did. Sitting on the bed, she followed him with her eyes, but did not move. She had reached the end of her tether. She had to know.

"Do you still love me?" she asked.

Ian stopped by the bed, looked at her quizzically, lifted her chin and kissed her lightly on the mouth. "People don't fly three thousand miles for no reason," he said, but broke away as she let her head fall against him. "Come on, let's explore!"

Had it always been like this? Sally asked herself miserably, as she explained about the ballroom and showed him the dark narrow stairway down and the one W.C. in the house.

"They call it the Lou," she said.

"I must remember that." But had it always been like this? Did it take a while for two people to find each other again? Had he changed? She couldn't have dreamt those kisses on which she had lived all these weeks. Why couldn't they talk? Why must she be so wary? For she felt hemmed in, prevented by some inner warning from forcing him into a corner.

Violet and Charles were nowhere to be seen. She and Ian stood in the hall and stared up at the portraits in silence.

"The gentry," he said, after a moment, ironically.

Then she led him into the unused part of the house, the empty drawing room. The sun was pouring in through the uncurtained high windows. A book lay open on the sofa, and an ashtray filled with cigarette stubs had been left on the floor beside it.

"I'm the only person who ever comes in here," Sally explained. "So Maire forgets the ashtray. It's my secret place. Just lately," she explained.

But Ian had walked right on through and now as he

turned the corner he gave a low whistle as if he had met a ghost.

"Oh, that's the old dining room. Victorian. Gloomy, isn't it?"

"This house is like Rome," Ian said, "layers and layers of periods laid on top of each other." He was excited now. "Where's all the furniture?"

"Oh, I don't know." Where was the furniture? She had never thought to ask. Actually she had grown to like its emptiness.

"This room is really splendid, you know," Ian said, dancing and watching himself dance a slow waltz in the mirror. "But it certainly could do with some paint, paper . . ." He stopped and made Sally a low bow.

"It's not like America," Sally said, unresponsive. "There just isn't any money here."

"It must be depressing," he said calmly. After all, it was no concern of his, Sally reminded herself.

"No," she withdrew into the recess of the window, "not if you live here."

"Why not? I think it's depressing that the Victorians did have the money." Ian sat down on the sofa, and somehow she minded his sitting there, lighting a cigarette so casually and flicking the match onto the floor, as if he were backstage somewhere and didn't care. "That's what would depress me if I lived here—seeing it go to pieces, living in the past."

"It's hard to explain," Sally said thoughtfully. "But after a while if you live here you don't see all those things, you forget about them. You just feel part of it.

You do what you can, you keep it alive—and that seems important, like Annie downstairs. It's her whole life. She loves the house. We all do," Sally ended, but she had not been convincing. She had not found the words. It was hard against Ian's detachment, to find them.

"Maybe, but there's no future in it." Ian sounded so glib that Sally was silenced. What future has a New York skyscraper? she wanted to say. "I thought you weren't going to like it here," he added crossly.

Sally caught her breath. Was he jealous of the house, of all this, even of her aunt and uncle? Was that it? She wanted now desperately to get out of this spiral of arguing.

"You haven't told me anything," she said, sitting down beside him almost meekly, putting a tentative hand on his sleeve and then, as there was no response, withdrawing it.

"Oh," he said with a false casualness, "I think I may have a contract with MGM. In fact, it's pretty well settled, so I'll be going West in September and that's why I thought I'd better come over and see you. It may be a while . . ." He didn't look at her and pretended not to know what he was saying.

"How long?" Sally felt as if the whole world was blowing away. "Oh Ian—" she said and she meant, please, please look at me.

"It's the chance of a lifetime, Sally. If I should really get a break— Heavens, there's nothing I couldn't do. Come back to New York and choose my own plays . . ." He turned to her now, brilliant with anticipation, as if all this had no connection with "them," as if she must share his enthusiasm.

"Oh, how I hate being a woman," Sally said fiercely.

"I don't get it." Ian offered her a cigarette as if it was the only thing he could think of at the moment.

"No thanks." She sat staring out. "Women have to wait around and see what men will do first. They can never act on their own," she said bitterly.

"You'll be at college, won't you? It isn't as if . . ." but he didn't finish the sentence. They sat there in the big empty room, with the sunlight dazzling their eyes, in a vacuum of feeling. Irritation, tears, love would have to rush in in a moment, Sally felt; anything would be better than this emptiness all around and inside her.

But Ian looked at his watch. "Almost noon. Didn't your uncle say something about cocktails on the terrace? I'll go see . . ."

It was a deliberate evasion, a cruel one, depriving the moment of its climax, of its release. Sally felt madly frustrated. She could hear him talking to Uncle Charles in the hall, the clink of bottles and glasses, the glass door being opened and closed. Men are cowards, she thought. They won't face things. And then, Why had he come? It was finally a relief to go out on the terrace and to know that she could give up trying for a while. She lay down on the next to bottom step with a pillow under her head, smoking—their voices, like voices in a dream came to her, Violet laughing suddenly at something Charles said, Ian being fearfully polite and careful to say the right thing (faintly and from far away she was amused).

"Isn't the little mad thing drinking?" Uncle Charles stood above her, shutting out the sky. She closed her eyes and then sat up.

"Of course I am."

They were making plans for the afternoon. "Tweed," Ian was saying. He was saying "Irish whiskey." They were drinking up fast out of nervousness. Suddenly it felt hot. There wasn't a breath of wind in the radiant still air. Light sprang up at them from everywhere, reflected back even from the stone of the house. There was a sense of being becalmed, of having arrived nowhere in particular but being forced to stay there.

"We've heard so little about you." Violet took out her petit point as if preparing to listen to a long story. "Do tell us something—anything—I feel totally ignorant."

"He's going to Hollywood," Sally said. And because she was feeling a little drunk with anxiety, despair, the sun, the martini, she said, "He's going to be a movie star. He'll never come back."

"It's a wonderful contract, Mrs. Gordon," Ian ignored Sally. He was sitting cross-legged on a cushion at Violet's feet and now swung round, his back to the others as if he were pleading his case, "and of course the whole point is to get back to Broadway. It'll only be a year or two . . ."

Violet, who had suspected after one glance at Sally's attitude of definite withdrawal that things were not going very well, now glanced over at her anxiously.

"Two years sounds like an awfully long time," she said gently.

Sally got up, went over to a chair beside Charles, and sat down. She did not want to hear about all the glorious plans. She deliberately shut her attention off.

"Oh Charles," she said.

Charles was flattered by the intimacy of this spoken sigh.

"You're looking very beautiful today, did you know it?" he said rather shyly, not looking at her. What struck Sally was the goodness of this smiling middle-aged man, fumbling for the consoling thing to say as if he were looking for a shiny dime to lay in her hand. For I am a beggar, she thought, yes, I am a beggar. And I have been mean to Charles. It is Violet's fault, she thought. She should never have told me what she did. She should have let me find out, if it was necessary to find out.

"It's nice to be told one's beautiful even if one isn't —especially if one isn't. Violet, I should think, would get rather tired of it."

Charles chuckled. "You might think so, but she never does," he whispered, feeling rather superior.

"It's like a reflection. She sees herself through other peoples' eyes." Sally had just invented this and she was surprised at its truth, for as she glanced over at Violet and Ian, she saw that this was happening right before her. Violet had become animated, though she sat so quietly listening. It was as if a light had been turned on. Then, as if the two such a short distance away, yet so far, had sensed the weight of eyes upon them, Ian turned in the middle of a sentence and Violet looked up.

"Ian's been telling me about Texas, about his father . . ." she said to answer their question.

But, Sally thought, that is not really it. He has been really telling you that you are beautiful and so you are beautiful again. But what, she asked herself, have *you* been telling *him*, that is not in the words? For, Ian, she thought, is full of glitter and no woman could resist him when he is like this. It was as if they were alone in the blazing sunlight and she and Charles were forced into shadow by their brilliance. They are the beloved, she thought, and Charles and I are the lovers —yes, even if Charles is unfaithful to her, still . . .

It was clear to Sally suddenly that Ian and Violet who must always call out the feeling of others, did it not because they needed love as she did so desperately, but because they needed to be given back themselves, an entirely other thing. It was like a new hat or a new necktie that they could wear. She wondered how long they had been sitting there staring, how long the pause had taken before Maire came out to say that lunch was ready. Such enormous things happen in a few seconds. By the way Charles took her arm, she knew that he and she were allies now, that the whole kaleidoscope of relationships had shifted. There was a new pattern forming. And Sally was astonished to realize that she did not feel so much hurt as curious.

But though the kaleidoscope of feeling was being rather violently shaken up, the rites and forms of life in the house did not alter. Violet had insisted that she must be allowed to do the flowers in peace before they started out on their long drive to town and to the mountains the next morning. And now she was standing before the piles of snapdragons, their heads heavy with rain, before the few tall spires of larkspur she had been able to save, and the careful faces of the zinnias (rain did not crumple them!) spread out on damp newspapers, covering almost the whole of the table in the study. At her feet she threw the withered stalks from the bunch which had stood there gradually disintegrating for the last two days. Sometimes the fugitive nature of this work into which she put so much thought and care depressed Violet. This was one of those days. They fade so fast, she was thinking. But what a rest it was to be arranging these passive stalks and stems, what a refuge from life with people who never would stay put, who developed resentments and jealousies, or began to make demands just when one thought everything was settled. She had not slept very well. Charles had been peculiarly difficult, worrying the whole affair of Ian like a dog with a bone, growling at the bone of Ian, then burying it firmly, only to unbury it again ten minutes later. It was exasperating because she had no answers for Charles's questions. It was clear that Ian had not come on the tide of love, as they supposed. Why then had he come? What was the point of such a journey? And the queer thing was, she had thought, that here they were, four people thrown together in this house, and yet suddenly no two of us can communicate at all. The evening had seemed interminable. Charles, Ian and Sally played bridge and she did her petit point. The evening had been full of glances and pushes and prods, until they were all four as nervous as porcupines with all their quills on end, though nothing had been said, nothing had happened.

And now where were they? she asked herself, relieved that at least they were not here, and she could quietly build her bouquet, transitory as it would be. Yet it gave her a feeling of stability, of continuity—

"Mrs. Gordon?" The voice came from the back door of the library and she turned, startled.

"Oh good morning, Ian. Did you sleep well?" He looked absurdly young, she thought, in a white turtle neck sweater.

"Very well, thank you, though I found the stillness a bit nerve-wracking at first. There was some peculiar cry that came back several times—"

"Oh, the owl, I expect." She went back to her flowers with deliberation.

"I thought it was a ghost," he smiled. "I hoped it was."

"Where's Sally?" Violet asked. This was to prevent him from doing what he did, which was to settle on the arm of the sofa, leaning over the back of it where he could look up at her face. She didn't want to be looked at.

"She's gone off somewhere," he said indifferently. And then, "I want to talk to you, Mrs. Gordon."

"Do you?" Violet asked and the tone said, Whatever for? "Well," she said lightly but definitely, "the trouble is that I can't do this and talk at the same time. And as I have to do this . . ." Already she was ruining her plan out of nervousness. The larkspur was too tall—she needed more body. Deliberately she shut out the insistence of his look. She would not see him.

But as Ian was perfectly silent and just sat there, watching her, it became more difficult to go on than if they had been chatting about indifferent things. The silence was too much like intimacy.

"You're amazing," Ian said quietly, "I've never seen anyone like you before."

Violet couldn't help smiling. It was so clumsy and so indiscreet.

"What's funny?" he asked, his face aflame with insecurity.

"You make me sound like a specimen," she said, bending her head first to one side and then to another, as she began to stick the stiff zinnias into the gaps in the bunch. "As a matter of fact you look at us all rather like specimens, don't you, Ian?" she said wickedly. "You have been looking us over—that's only natural."

He got up, half angrily, his hands shoved into his pockets. "I don't know how to talk to you," he said, "you baffle me."

"You must be very easily baffled then. Besides," she added, very busy with the flowers, "I thought you came here to talk to Sally."

"That's just it," Ian broke in, "that's what I want to talk to you about."

"Oh." Violet stood behind the table and faced him, for the first time looking him full in the face. "Well, Ian, I am listening," she said.

"Don't look so severe, Mrs. Gordon." He was standing now back to the fireplace. "I'm not a criminal."

"Have I said you were?"

"Oh dear, this is awful." Ian ran a hand through his hair and seemed genuinely upset. But Violet did not feel sorry for him. She suspected that he was out for sympathy and understanding, a special kind of sympathy and understanding which could only be had from a woman about another woman. She was not prepared to give this.

"You see," Ian began, lighting a cigarette and smoking nervously without inhaling, little puffs of smoke flowing out of his mouth between the words, "Sally's such a child." He looked at Violet for confirmation of this.

"She's twenty-one," Violet said, without committing herself.

"That's not what I mean. She takes things so hard. She thinks everything's black and white, one thing or another."

"I'm afraid I don't follow."

"I can't marry Sally," Ian said almost angrily.

"Why not?" Violet pressed him, and as he didn't answer, but stood there frowning, a frown so handsome and *voulu* that Violet, who recognized some of her own bad habits, knew at once that he was not thinking at all, but only being something, being a handsome frowning young man who hoped she found him attractive in this guise.

"Are you in love with Sally, or not?" Violet's voice was like ice.

"I thought I was." There was this about Ian, Violet had to admit. He surprised one sometimes by being a little more honest than one expected.

"What happened, Ian?" and this time her tone was kind.

"I don't know. When I saw her at the airport and later here in this house—I don't know—it was as if something snapped. Oh, I don't know what I feel," he said harshly. "I shouldn't have come."

"Oh no, that's not true. You *should* have come," Violet said gravely.

"You know what it is," he pleaded now, "*you're* loved. You know what it is, how sometimes you just can't stand it any longer, as if you couldn't breathe—that's how I feel, Mrs. Gordon."

She had never said it to herself like that, no, perhaps she had never felt it.

"I think I do know," Violet said, coming round and sitting down in one of the armchairs. "When it comes to the real thing, one can't take it."

Ian smiled. "You're being rather cruel, Mrs. Gordon."

"Only to myself," she said quickly.

"How is she being cruel, Ian?" Sally's light harsh voice interrupted them. She stood in the big doorway, Ian at the fireplace on her left and Violet opposite her.

"Ian and I are telling each other a few unpleasant truths," Violet said quickly.

"She hates to be interrupted while she's doing the flowers," Sally said and turned and went out.

The impact of this sudden entrance and exit was such that there was no way of going on. Violet went back to the flowers, re-arranging them now with almost vicious efficiency. She rolled up the wet newspapers, flung a bunch of broken stems into the wastebasket, and said with every gesture, Go away. But Ian did not go away. He just stood there, looking at her, his eyes narrowed, like an animal, she thought, like a cat with its ears back, about to spring.

"You will have to say all this to Sally," Violet said finally. "You must say it to her, not to me."

"Don't shut me out," he pleaded.

But Violet was already moving deliberately toward the door.

"You're not quite honest, you know," she said with her back to him.

"How did you know?" He looked so relieved that it was almost like happiness. He was, she felt, ready and willing to confide. It was what he had really come down here to do. But she would not have it. She would not be his ally, know his truth too well, whatever it might be. She was a little afraid of him because he showed her at every moment the worst of herself. She would not be led any further down the mirrored corridors to whatever monster or Minotaur she would be forced to kill if she found him.

"Never mind," she said, not unkindly. "I've lived a long time." And then she closed the door behind her and went upstairs, annoyed to discover that she was shaking as if she had escaped some peril. Sally was sitting on the window seat on the landing, also like a little tense animal. We are all animals, Violet thought with something like disgust.

"Go down to Ian. It's you he wants to see," she said quietly.

"Yes." Sally ran down the stairs, the violence of her feeling forcing her on like an arrow that has left the bow. She flung open the door and then stood quite still just inside. "Why did you come here, Ian?" she asked, as if she were facing a burglar or a criminal.

"What's the matter with you, Sally? Why are you so

angry all of a sudden?" He stood there, looking down, evading her eyes, immaculate and untouched in his white sweater, as if she were the incomprehensible one.

"You know what I mean," Sally said in the same relentless tone. "Why did you? Because you thought it would be amusing to see a house like this? Because you were curious? Or just for the hell of it?" She came a few steps towards him. "You've got to answer," she said. Her face was quite frightening.

Then all of a sudden she collapsed into the chair beside her, covered her face with her hands and said very quietly, "You know what you've been doing, I suppose —the suspense—"

"Oh Sally . . ." She heard the evasion in the tone, apologetic, faintly exasperated.

"You've got to tell me," Sally said, her hands in fists held against her eyes. "I can't stand it any longer."

It was clear that she was reaching the ultimate tautness of a thread that has been pulled out as far as it will go and now at any second must break. It was approaching a scream, hysteria, or (this is what she thought herself) death.

"I can't help it, Sally. It's not my f-f-fault." He was stammering with nerves himself.

"If you could just try to tell me," she pleaded, "if I could just *know* . . ."

"I didn't mean it to be like this," he faltered. "Actually," he said (as if he were discussing a dinner engagement, she thought), "I had a wild idea we might get married—here—away from your father and mother and

—everything—but, oh, Sally, try to understand. Don't hate me." He had turned away from her. He would always meet a difficult situation obliquely, Sally thought, as she examined him coldly, his weakness. He looked much older as if the sheen had rubbed off. He's thirty, she thought. He should be something by now.

"What if I do hate you?" She was not going to pity him. It was indecent of him to expect her pity. "That would be better than this. I hate myself now," she added in a low voice, as if to herself, "I'm becoming a monster." When someone doesn't love you, you become a monster, she was thinking. It takes yourself away, like a dreadful disease. It seemed incredible that she could have become in a few days this dry screaming harpy, unable even to cry.

"No, Sally darling, but . . ." Still he hesitates, she thought. Still he can't come towards me.

"But you don't love me any more. What is it then? I'm the same person. You did love me"—her voice trembled as the wave of doubt rose in her—"didn't you?"

Ian, driven finally into a corner, sat down, his hands clasped between his knees. "I guess," he said with a look of fear, of blank evasion in his eyes, like a goat, or some animal who cannot bear the straight human glance. "I guess I just can't take love. It scares me."

"Oh," Sally caught her breath. "You're the monster, then," she said harshly. "Why do you begin things you can't finish?"

"I didn't know," he said irritably, "I didn't know this would happen."

For the moment Sally was saved from suffering by anger. Also anger made her seize on the first weapon that came to mind, the way Ian behaved with her aunt, the mixture of deference when he was with her and irony when he spoke of her—she seized on this. "It's Aunt Violet," she said amazed at the poison welling up inside her. "You can never see a woman like that, a real woman who knows all the things you don't know without wanting to attack her, call her fossil or extinct or something, but at the same time you want to capture her. You can't resist, can you, Ian?" He lifted his head, shocked by her tone, the violence of her imagining and the core of truth in it. "Oh, you'll never admit it," she went on, "and nothing will come of it, of course," she added, "but that's the truth. It's always been the truth."

"No." Ian got up, for the first time forceful. "You're mad, Sally, and mean too. I never would have expected that of you."

They were both relieved to be angry. It distracted them from the real pain that lay under this false anger.

"I'm so tired of being myself," she said in a suddenly normal tone of voice.

This plea not directed to him, not asking anything of him at last made it possible for Ian to go over and sit on the arm of her chair. He put an arm round her, gently, with real tenderness. "You're so young, Sally dear, this can't be fatal."

"But how does one learn? How am I ever to get to be like Aunt Violet if nobody loves me whom I can love? It's hopeless. Damn," she said as she felt she would cry, and instead got up, running into Charles at the door. Luckily he was too concentrated on departure to notice her state.

"Tell Violet I'll be back with the car in ten minutes. Half the morning's gone and we really must be off."

Ian was left alone in the library. He went over and stood by the flowers on the table, looking at them with curiosity and great attention. It would have been hard to tell from his expression whether the scene he had just lived through had touched him deeply or disturbed him, or whether he had already put it out of his mind as something finished. At any rate, his attitude, hands in pockets, suggested relief.

They gathered on the terrace, Ian carrying Violet's coat on his arm, Violet, nervous, tying and retying a violet scarf round her neck, and Sally expressionless, keeping rather obviously in the background. The drive had taken on the atmosphere of an expedition. They were all glad to be getting out, to be forced to look at something other than themselves, to be immunized by flowing landscapes and unknown places from the concentrated feelings of the last twenty-four hours. For Sally, at least, the suspense at its worst was over. She was so relieved that she hardly knew or cared what she would feel later—now it was the passive calm one rests in after a violent fit of seasickness. She slipped gladly into the back seat with Violet.

"Charles will want to explain everything to Ian, you know, and it's so frightening when he has to turn round to do it." Then, as Charles slammed the door and got into the driver's seat, affairé, efficient, as if the little car were a plane, and some danger to be met and dealt with just ahead, Violet said in her teasing voice, "Darling, if you see some rare sort of nuthatch in a hedge behind you, please resist the irresistible and don't turn round. Bird-lovers should not be allowed licenses," she said, settling back, with a sigh.

Sally was not listening. She felt as if she were being lifted out of and away from everything familiar, as if in fact they were leaving the whole past behind them, and this were the beginning of a wholly new, strange life.

"All right?" Violet asked, slipping an arm through hers.

"Yes, thank you, Aunt Violet," she smiled stiffly. She did not know if it was the truth. But she was grateful for Aunt Violet's arm. It is awfully important, she thought, that I be loved by someone, right now.

Ian got out to open and close the gate and then they were really off. The sky was overcast, broken big clouds with radiant edges, and pools of sunlight on the far-off hills, a sky like changeable silk which bore watching every moment. Always coming out of the demesne there was this feeling of the world opening out, of adventure as the tarred road flowed sinuously off up and down hills as far as one could see.

"It's beautiful," Sally cried. "How beautiful it all is!" She knew that her eyes were opened, that she would never never forget a single thing they saw on this day. It all had such reality suddenly, such brilliance because —here she withdrew her arm from her aunt's—she had broken out of a shell. She had come alive. Such brilliance, she guessed, was part of suffering, of being aware —would she feel it if Ian were not still there in the front seat?

Here the fields were divided by rough stone walls; up on a hill silhouetted against the sky was the ruin of a castle covered with ivy, and then already it was past and they were running along beside a small still river with rushes in its bed.

"Not navigable," Charles pronounced, and Sally caught Violet's amused smile.

The voices of the two men rose and fell; Violet and Sally in the back were glad not to have to talk.

"We'll go right up to the hills, Violet, eh? Never mind the town. We can swing round there later. I want to catch this light."

Indeed it seemed as if they were in the middle of an iridescent bubble and every color of meadow, of deeper green hillside and far-off the purple mountains seemed touched with a peculiar and transitory brilliance. Each little flower by the road, a buttercup or a lacy head of Queen Anne's lace, seemed outlined carefully like flowers in the medieval paintings at the feet of the saints, Sally thought.

"I know what it is," she said, "it's that all the common things become magic here, that pig for instance, so very pink," she giggled, "and the grass really too green to be real. I wish I were a cow," she added, as they passed a herd, knee-deep in buttercups, lifting heavy heads, flowers dripping from their mouths.

Just then the sun fell on their necks as the road took a turn to the west, fell so warmly that it was like a caress. The hills which had been a dark deep blue changed to mauve and purple and seemed to shine.

Was it the sun on her neck, that warmth stealing through her so beneficently, or what was it? Sally felt as elated as if she were full of good news, bursting with some great tidings. She felt free to say all sorts of mad things.

"I love you all extremely," she announced, "I'm in love with three people. It's rather odd."

Charles turned half-round to see her and winked. It was his idea that she and Ian must have come to some understanding and he was so pleased for her that he forgot to be jealous.

"Charles!" Violet admonished. "Try to resist the birds and the beauties!"

"I just wanted to say hello to my niece. There's nothing on the road."

"Except two carts—Charles!" Violet shouted, as he just missed a cart, swerving out dangerously to the left and just not falling into a ditch.

"Violet doesn't drive," Charles explained to Ian, "and unfortunately she is very imaginative."

"Charles, unfortunately drives, and is very unimaginative," Violet countered, quite cross because she had been frightened. They were off on one of their games of crossness, and while they enjoyed themselves, Ian turned to smile tentatively at Sally. As long as he is here, she thought, I shall not know what has happened. Despair, she understood now, for a while is as exhilarating as joy. One is sustained by it.

Violet was puzzled, puzzled by Sally's air of exaltation, wondering what Ian had finally told her, or if he had told her. She thought that it would be nice when she and Charles were alone again, and she could sit in the front seat, and they could talk about nothing in peace.

They were climbing, past small stone houses with sills and doors painted green, past a man alone in a field mowing, the long slow sweep of the scythe laying the tall grass low, one step following another, one sweep following another in unbroken rhythm, and behind him nothing but meadows and hedges rolling off into sky.

"It looks easy, you know," Charles nodded in the man's direction, "but have you ever handled a scythe?"

"Of course Ian's never handled a scythe," Sally said scornfully. "He only handles a make-up stick."

Ian, put on his mettle, began to drum in time to the

215

scythe on the dashboard, his feet syncopating the slow rhythm. Then he hummed softly a little tune he was making up as he went along. "I can do it, though," he said after a few moments, "in my own way."

"Oh you're pretty wonderful," Sally granted. Just then the road dipped down, circled the bump of a hill and climped steeply. They were suddenly on a great height. The river looked now like a blue ribbon laced round the fields and the whole landscape a pattern which they could read. Charles slowed down and then stopped.

"A breath of air?" he asked. "A look round? Worth seeing," he said, already stuffing tobacco into his pipe. "You can see three counties from this height. In the old days in the carriage it took half a day, didn't it, Violet? It was a journey up here."

Violet was standing, blinking in the full sun, feeling deliciously relaxed and even a little drunk.

"Where's Dene's Court?" Sally asked. For what did all this landscape mean, and all the little farms and cut-up meager fields without that grandeur and space, and the tall stone house?

Charles took her arm and walked her a few yards up the road. "It's only trees from here," he said. "The house is entirely hidden. But look—see that grove there, the patches of darkness—just back of them, that should be the house." He was looking at her as she peered down, rather nervously as if she was afraid it might get lost if she didn't find it with her eyes.

"How's my favorite niece?" he asked, slipping an arm

through hers and puffing comfortably at his pipe, held in the other hand.

"The patient is resting comfortably," she said and then, "Oh, Uncle Charles. I think it's all over. I think it never was."

Charles, who had imagined that all was well, was so startled that he could do nothing but make a little distressed noise that sounded like "tut."

"Nonsense, you must be dreaming," he said gruffly when he had recovered. His own relief was so great he found, that he could not trust it. "We've got quite fond of him, you know. I'm sorry to hear it," he said, feeling embarrassed and wondering if they were being watched, wondering if Violet knew. "But it's not fatal," he added, giving her a rather penetrating look, for indeed she seemed very much intact.

"That's just what Ian said. What is it, Uncle Charles, that you all know that I don't know, that you all have that I don't have? I feel so queer, like an orphan—or a leper—why does nobody tell me what's wrong?"

"Nothing's wrong," Charles said emphatically, and he gave her arm a squeeze.

So much feeling had been dammed up in Sally for so long that this warm, loving pressure made her shiver, and quickly withdraw her arm. She did not really like the feeling she had, but now she found herself watching Charles's hands; he was pointing out the smoke of the town in the distance, a steeple, and very far-off just a thin line of blue, some mountains with a tremendously long peculiar name. She hardly listened. She looked at him. After dealing with Ian who slid about like a fish, whose element might be air or water but was surely not earth, there was peace in contemplating Charles, his firm dense head, with its close-cropped hair, his air of physical mastery as he stood surveying the landscape, above all his hands, tense hands which never made a tentative gesture.

Meanwhile Violet and Ian had walked off a little way down the road to look at another county. Violet was voluble, for once. She wanted to avoid confessions and pleas for mercy and attention. Also, coming up here so swiftly, the landscape given them like a sudden present had brought back her childhood as if in a dream. It was like a dream to come up here so very quickly, the journey which had taken half a day, which really should take half a day.

"We used to come up here about twice a year, when we were children, always in the late spring and then again in the autumn. In summer it was apt to be too hot, and also there were so many other things to do. Once after we got up here, the weather changed and it snowed. We were nearly frozen, but oh how lovely it was—like a Chinese landscape, the black hedges and the green fields frosted over. Only the horses didn't like it much and we were at the age when animals matter much more than people, so it ended by being agonizing, slippery, you know. And then Father got into an awful temper because Flaherty, the coachman, blamed him for starting out in the first place. We were so cold and Barbie was furious, I remember, because I cried."

"You don't seem like sisters at all," Ian said. "It's most improbable—"

"I haven't seen her for years, you know. I wonder if she's changed . . ." Here on the height where childhood melted into the present moment, it seemed amazing, cruel, that she had not seen her sister for over twenty years. "She should have come back," Violet said quite severely. "It's not right."

"Why doesn't she? Is there a mystery about it?" Ian said. And Violet was irritated that he could pay so much more attention to her than to the great glory of the country, this high point to which one made a yearly pilgrimage.

"No mystery—she was unhappy here. We never got on." The tone was forbidding. Ian lit a cigarette, after offering her one, which she refused, saying "Let's go back. Charles will be impatient."

"Only one more day," Ian said, as if the idea were tragic.

"I doubt if Sally could bear more than that," Violet answered. At that moment they looked up and saw Sally and Charles laughing. It was disconcerting. It did not fit in with what had happened that morning. She looked, Violet thought, more attractive than ever, eager, a little wild as if there were no care in the world—as if, Violet saw suddenly, there were no one in the world but Charles who was clearly basking, who felt like a lord of creation, clearly.

"She seems rather cheerful."

"You're a fool," Violet said crossly.

"I don't know why you're so cruel," Ian was smiling as if she had paid him a compliment. Perhaps he felt he had scored. "I was just stating a fact, on the evidence—"

"Why am I so mean to you?" Violet looked at him for the first time since they had wandered off. "Do you really want to know?" And now she smiled at him, a mischievous, and yet not a personal smile. "I think it's because I know you too well. I see in you my every weakness, my every vice."

This for the moment silenced Ian. Apparently it was not what he had expected at all.

"You are the most amazing person, Violet," he murmured. And then "Don't run away. They're perfectly happy. There's so much I want to ask you—and there's so little time . . ." he pleaded. He saw her hesitate and quickly pinned her down by going on, forcing her to pay attention to him in spite of herself by speaking rapidly in a low voice, a trick he used unconsciously, but it worked. Violet was looking at him instead of at the landscape at last.

"You said I wasn't honest. It's quite true. What made me come was you—you see, Sally kept writing about you," he went on without seeming to notice Violet's gesture of denial, the narrowing of her eyes. "Her letters were full of you and the house. I simply *had* to come," he said, with the complete unconsciousness of the person who sees only what he wants, and sees it with great intensity.

"But I don't understand." Violet really was too surprised to be less than honest. Then it came over her that it was disturbing to have those letters written, those letters all about her, this invasion of her house, her privacy, her marriage. "Whatever did Sally say?" The minute she had asked the question, she regretted it. She was giving him an inch, and now she looked away.

But Ian was alight with his victory. "Oh," he said airily, "that you were superficial, that you were a great beauty, that you were much too good for Charles—"

"She had no business to write such letters," Violet was suddenly angry. It was just too much, these intolerably young selfish children prying into her life, making something of it. It was none of their business.

"Well, of course she was obviously mad about you," Ian went on, apparently enjoying himself thoroughly. "That's what I read between the lines. So, it was only natural, wasn't it, that I come and see for myself—after all . . ." It was clear that all this was intoxicating to him; Violet could almost see the flames of curiosity licking around him as if he were a salamander and loved the fire. He had come, she sensed, because he was drawn to any situation which had complications, because he could not resist theater, even in life.

"And what did you think would happen?" Violet asked. "Did it occur to you that Sally might not guess your reasons for coming? That you were behaving like an utter cad?"

"Oh, Violet," he said half-laughing, "it's so easy to throw words like that around."

"It's easy if they don't mean anything." Far off down the road, she saw Charles and Sally walking, their heads bent, a little apart, yet apparently so absorbed in what they were saying that they had forgotten the view, the place, had forgotten, so it seemed, herself and Ian. And she had the illusion that she and Ian were in another world, hell or purgatory perhaps, and they were far off in another circle, one of the heavenly circles where the innocent may walk. For once more she was being forced to bear the guilt her beauty created for her, and she created for herself, for hadn't she after all wanted to charm Sally, to charm Ian? Hadn't this been her intention? But was it her fault if they ran away with casual presents and made them into secret treasures, magnified them and the giver, they who knew nothing of love? "If you came all this way out of curiosity, I hope you found whatever you were looking for," she said acidly.

"I found you, but I don't understand you," Ian said quietly. "At one moment you seem to understand everything and tease me about our being alike, fellow sinners so to speak, and the next you're standing off like some aloof goddess, feeling infinitely superior apparently. It's rather disconcerting."

"Yes," Violet said drily, "no doubt it's meant to be."

"Besides I haven't broken Sally's heart," he said almost crossly.

"I don't think we'll any of us know that, she less than anyone else, until you've gone." Then Violet walked away down the hill, and left Ian standing there. She had decided that she had had enough. She wanted, she needed to be with Charles who did not make her feel like a criminal.

"We'll be dreadfully late for lunch, Charles," she called impatiently. "We'll have to put off going to town till this afternoon."

"Oh well," Charles said, as they settled in again, two by two, as the doors slammed, as they took a last look at the still landscape before it would begin to move, "that doesn't matter. This was the great thing, to get the view, wasn't it, Sally?"

"Oh yes," Sally answered with a vague smile, "the view."

No one talked much on the way home. The climb up had matched a climbing mood of elation, and now they were going down, the mood ebbed. Ian smoked one cigarette after another. Sally had withdrawn into her corner. Violet wondered how on earth she would get through the next twenty-four hours without a tête-à-tête with Ian. If he were only leaving now, she thought, tonight.

The car ground to a stop on the gravel and once more Ian sprang out to open and close the gate as they passed through. It's like a spell, Sally was thinking, that closing of the gate. All the dimensions change. The land becomes intimate and so much smaller than outside, and the house becomes enormous. She had forgotten Ian. When he climbed back in he seemed like an intruder.

Perhaps he felt this for as the house appeared round the curve, narrow, high, seen from the side, he giggled and said nervously, "I see why you thought it looked like a prison, Sally."

"Did I?" She was astonished at his meanness. "I don't remember." For surely he had meant it, to make her feel that she did not belong. Yet as she got out of the car and looked up at the high windows, at the green light of the leaves reflected in them, she felt terribly lonely. It is not a prison, she thought, but it is not home either. It's too disturbing. It asks too much. Or our lives are too small to fill it.

She ran up the terrace steps, through the dining hall, past all the portraits which she felt but did not stop to look at; she ran up the great staircase to the landing, round the corner and up the narrow dark stairs to the empty sun-flooded ballroom. Here she stopped, wondering what she had been running away from, what she had been running towards. The surf of tears was rising again. But I've cried too much here, Sally thought sternly, altogether too much. It's indecent to cry so much, to well over like a leaky teapot. I'm never going to cry again, she said, walking up and down clasping her hands together as if to stop the rising flood. They were not tears for herself or for Ian or Violet, but for something much bigger than any of them, and she was afraid if she once began that she would never be able to stop at all. Once let these tears in and she would not be able to see; all would become muddy and obscure, dragging her down. But what she demanded now of herself was a cold clear light, clarification by the intellect.

She looked at the unfinished ceiling, walked the full length of the ballroom once more and then stood at the low windows and looked down at the sheep nibbling the rough grass. The breathless seizure by anguish that had driven her up here was past. We can't be heroes, she thought. Even the house never stood for heroics; that's why Sarah St. Leger doesn't fit in quite. We have to find the way to be human without disintegrating into messy little feelings. We have to be human on a grand scale like Annie, maybe. It was Sally's good-bye to Ian, because she knew now he was everything except quite human, a little golden idol she had worshipped like a pagan. But the true faith she saw, meant the breaking of idols—even Aunt Violet, even perhaps the house which if it was anything, was a living organism—breathing the open and stopped diapason of human lives, sounding its music through them, just as they were supported by it. The house provided a form for the chaotic hours, the changes of time and feeling; but without these changes it would die.

Standing at the window, Sally came as near perhaps as anyone does to a vision of life. By mastering feeling, she had come to understand the meaning of discipline and its reward: freedom and power.

The next morning she climbed the hill with Ian, for he would not go of course without making the classic walk to the classic view of Dene's Court. They stumbled on tussocks of thick grass, watching the sheep O'Neil had finally brought over stare at them and then dash off in groups, never able to make up their minds singly, driven together if at all.

"Such stupid animals," Sally said as if it were their fault and they might at least try to be more intelligent.

"I should never have come." Ian walked with his head down, seeing nothing. "I've ruined everything."

"Aunt Violet doesn't like you very much, if that's what you mean," Sally said drily. She had not meant to be cruel, but found she could not help it.

"Of course that's not what I mean."

"I wonder if you know what you mean," Sally became gentle. "You've got to want one thing more than anything else, to know."

"I want to be a good actor," Ian said vehemently. "I

want to know everything about people," and then he turned and faced her, "Why did you say that about your aunt?"

Sally laughed a funny dry laugh which it hurt to do. "Because it's true. Now that I've been able to separate you from myself I see that you're like a chameleon. Ever since you've come, Ian, you haven't been real for a moment. I'm clumsy, I bungle, and fall down. I don't fit in, but at least I'm real," Sally said with a kind of triumph. She turned away to go on climbing the hill, doggedly. Ian followed a few steps behind. Kicking a tussock, he nearly stumbled.

When she looked back she saw him against the unyielding stone face of the house. He was standing there, small and frail, obviously undecided whether to be angry or not, and as she watched he looked up and met her gaze for a second before he looked away, frowning. Even two days before she would have been drawn as if by a magnet to touch this face where so many things were written so quickly, so intensely, and then erased. But now what she saw was the house behind him and she knew that what she wanted above all was to marry and to have children and to bring her children here. And this wish had nothing now to do with Ian who was some extreme private enterprise in which nothing for a time had existed or could exist except her feeling for him, a feeling all in the present, having no future before it. But if he had kissed me, she thought with terror, would I have known all this?

Just then Violet and Charles came out on the terrace

and waved. Sally watched them, and watched Ian wave back excitedly, and it reminded her of the time long ago when she had come here with Charles. Then the house and she had seemed pitted against each other and the house was her enemy.

"There," she said as Ian stood beside her, panting from the climb, "there it is."

"But look at Violet and Charles," Ian was excited. "Don't they look lovely standing there?"

"Yes," Sally was impatient, "but the point is the house. Do really look at it, Ian, please do," she entreated him as if it was suddenly important that he know, that he see.

"It looks awfully grim to me," he shivered, and then looked at her curiously, possessed as she was by some strange elation, as if she held power in her hands and this power was in some way communicated by the house. "I thought anyway it was Violet you loved, not the house."

"You know," she turned to him with relief as if they had become two people again, not lovers, not antagonists, but people who could look into each other's eyes, "I thought so too."

"Well, why doesn't that make a chameleon of you?" He smiled his winner's smile at her and she smiled back right into his eyes.

"Because I know now what I want." She looked down at the house and nodded as if she were making a promise. Then she ran down ahead of him. "I'll race you!" she called back, knowing that as she ran away from him, forever, she had become again desirable, though it did not matter.

She really ran away, told him off—"Aunt Violet's probably in the walled garden"—did not even wait to see what his reaction would be, though she heard him call, "Sally, where are you?" once in the great hall, and then not call again.

When the coast was clear, she went into the library and stood at the desk. There was something, she felt, waiting to pounce whenever she was inactive now. It was there in the landscape before her, lying there peaceful and self-contained, the indifferent sheep and the indifferent trees. It was alarming and soothing at the same time. It's because, she thought, I'm on my own now. There is no one. I'm free. In the walled garden, she thought, Violet and Ian are entangled by their feelings, Violet warding him off, Ian trying to get under her armor. It was strange to discover that she did not mind. But just then she saw Charles coming down the road with his long easy stride, and the landscape came alive again and had a human element and this she could not resist. For she had, she realized now, been dreadfully lonely for the last ten minutes. In a second she was out of the door and on the terrace waving. Because she was free, because she was alone, she felt a deep drive towards everyone she loved simply. It was as if she only existed in the presence of others, anything else was still too frightening. She could not wait for Charles on the terrace—she must run to meet him, out of breath, smiling so much from so far off that she felt her mouth crack at the sides.

"Oh, Charles," she said with a deep sigh, "oh, there you are."

She stood before him smiling and smiling, and he stopped and smiled back.

"What's happened?" he asked. "What's the hurry?"

"Oh nothing—I saw you—"

"I've been up in the wood with the men."

"I know."

To be loved, she thought. She thought, safety. Charles saw the look in her eyes, so open, so wide-open and vulnerable, and a week ago this look would have made the blood pound through his body in exultation. A week ago he would have kissed her; he wouldn't have been able to resist. But Charles too had changed, had grown, had passed into a new phase. It was not so much that he felt old now (he had felt old then when he imagined that he wanted her), but more that he saw her youth and all its implications and was moved by it for itself, as if she were his own child. He put an arm round her shoulder,

"It's nearly lunch time. Where are the others?"

There were no signs of a struggle in the walled garden where the espaliered peaches were just turning a deep rose and the pears, still green, hung in little clusters like enormous grapes. It was rather like being in a huge open greenhouse, so warm and damp was it there, with a haze of bees over the flowers and a deep continual buzz. There were no signs of a struggle. Violet's gloves, her gardening basket and another flatter one filled with roses, stood in the path. But Ian had had to fight to get her to come and sit down on the bench, and she had only given in because he seemed about to become violent, and what was the use of a scene at this point?

So she sat, very erect beside him, in a pose so formal that she looked as if someone were taking her photograph. She had, it seemed, set up her whole physical being like a screen. And she did not turn her eyes in Ian's direction, as she listened.

"Don't you see? Can't you understand?" he was saying "I thought I loved her. Hasn't that ever happened to you?"

Violet just inclined her head. Indeed indeed it had happened and she had more than once when she was young imagined that such concentrated attention must be contagious, had thought because she was loved that she must be in love.

"She used to come on to New York for weekends—she was so eager and darling and so different from all the ambitious self-centered slightly overdeveloped women I knew in the theater, overdeveloped like an overdeveloped film I mean, their personalities so dreadfully underlined. She made everything seem wonderful . . ."

"Including you," Violet said gently.

"Of course including me. Everything we did was magic—it really was," he protested, as he saw the shadow of a smile on the aloof beautiful face turned away from him. "You don't believe me."

"Of course I believe you. But then what happened?" Now she turned and looked at him once curiously, intently. "The mirror broke, did it? You couldn't find your reflection any more? Why not?" Now she was really interested suddenly. "For she hadn't changed—"

"I don't know," Ian looked off, pressing the palms of his hands together as if he were locking something up inside him. "I don't know, Violet—it's too complicated. You see all her letters were full of you. I was jealous at first, a little—then I began to feel curious, then I felt I had to see you myself. Then . . ." he stopped and looked at her almost humbly, and Violet realized how young he was, with all his airs and graces, how much he needed to be liked, how vulnerable.

"Then?" But she was smiling now, what he read as an indulgent smile. At last she was listening to him as if he were a real person.

"Then I found out that innocence is both terrible and boring." Now he had said it, he was afraid she would be angry.

Instead Violet sighed. "Yes. The mirror was too honest and too clear and perhaps too deep. It gave you back things you didn't want to know about yourself, didn't it?"

"I do think love is frightening," Ian said wincing, as if at a blow. "It scares me. I don't want to be needed that much."

"You don't really want to live, do you, Ian? You want to act. They seem to be quite different things."

"But how can I act if I don't live?" He turned on her almost angrily. "I've got to know people, people like you for instance. I've got to have a chance to learn," he said passionately as if he were making love to her.

"People are hardly objects you can pick up and take to pieces to find out how they tick. You're dangerous, Ian, you're a menace," she said gravely. "What you haven't learned is that people with your charm are always in debt to life, Ian—we never quite pay it back." She was unconscious of the change in pronoun. "You can't *use* people. It's too dangerous."

"You do make me feel like a cad," he said ruefully, but she knew as well as he did that as long as he had her attention, nothing she could say now would hurt, even if it did later. He was basking. "I wish I knew more about you and what has made you what you are." This was a gentler tone, and it surprised Violet into honesty.

"But I'm nothing," she sounded dismayed, "nothing at all, Ian. Sally's fifty times the person I'll ever be."

"Why? I don't see that. I don't."

"She asks more of life, of herself, of everyone around her than either you or I ever will. She looks at all this," she said, letting her eyes rest on the trellised banks of sweet peas, "and wants to know what it all means. She never stops asking questions about things as they are in themselves. There's a deep realistic root to her romanticism and that gives it validity. I have great respect for Sally," she ended.

"So I gather." Ian was perhaps ashamed. But Violet seemed to have forgotten him. "All my life I've felt guilty," she said suddenly.

The last thing she had expected was to find herself confiding in Ian, but now she had begun, the moment held her and she must go on. Perhaps it was that Ian would be leaving and never come back, so she would not be called to account for what she said. Perhaps it was that she had truly recognized her buried self in him, herself as she might have been if she had not married

Charles who had forced her both by his strength and his weakness to grow and to endure and to understand because she really loved him. "Don't you see that it's a frightful thing you've done to me—all this? That it's brought back all the old guilt, the repeated pattern. I can't believe quite that I'm responsible for what has happened between you and Sally, but it has happened before so it frightens me—not through my will, Ian, believe me . . ."

"I do believe you," he said quietly. "I'm terribly sorry, Violet. Can you, will you ever forgive me?"

"Don't be a fool," she said harshly. "It's myself I can't forgive."

"I don't see why. It's not your fault if you weave a spell, if people have to love you."

"Yes," Violet answered in a low voice, "it is my fault. In my heart of hearts, I suppose I want to be loved. You only call out of people what you want to call out. It doesn't just happen. That's the guilt," she said, putting one hand on his. "And now," she said, getting up, as if this small gesture had been too much. "It's time we found Charles and Sally. It's time," she said with a delightful cool smile, "that we rejoined the innocents."

Ian for once was speechless. He felt as if too much had been given him all at once, but he was darned if he knew quite what it was.

Charles and Sally were waiting for them on the terrace, Charles relaxed in his usual rattan chair, Sally as
usual hunched up on a cushion on the steps. They
looked peaceful and solid, so that for a second Violet had
the sensation that she and Ian were immaterial, were
ghosts. Then Sally raised her head. There was too much
pain, open and alive, in her face. It struck Violet a hard
hurting blow, so hard she stopped where she was.

"Hello there, have we been gone long?" as if indeed
she and Ian had been gone hours instead of a half-hour
at most.

"Have your ears been burning?" Ian asked Sally, running up the steps quickly, eagerly as if he were bringing
a present.

She did not look at him. She just shook her head, a
slow deep blush mounting through her neck.

"We've been talking about you, haven't we, Violet?"

He turned to find the Violet he had just met in the
garden, but she was no longer there. What he met was

236

a cold refusing glance. In the second of silence that followed his question, as it lay there unanswered, he may have felt some final parting taking place. He was now absolutely outside the group. They would stay on here. But in a few hours he would be halfway up the sky, moving faster than time to the other side of the world. He sat down beside Sally on the step, his arms hugging his knees. How long was this pause in which the kaleidoscope of feeling would one last time be shaken and take its pattern? None of them could have measured it in seconds or minutes.

But in it Violet slowly climbed the steps and sat down in her round-backed sheltering chair, and looked over at Charles and found his eyes and rested there a second, answering all his questions in a single look. No, she said to him, it is not what you and Sally think, not that at all. It is something else, her look told him. It told him, what matters, what always matters above all is us, Charles.

In it Sally slowly lifted her head and caught Violet's exchange, the silent exchange of understanding with her husband. It was as if she had been holding her breath under water and at last could come up for air. The wild revolving pieces of life were settling again into a pattern, and she sighed.

"What did you say about me?" she asked Violet, ignoring Ian completely.

This was the fourth question that had lain on the air but this time Violet laughed her charmed, her slightly theatrical laugh and said, "Darling, if we told you we'd

237

turn your head and that would be a pity, wouldn't it, Charles?"

Charles grunted a noncommittal answer. Then got up, yawned and stretched like a large comfortable cat, Violet thought, and said, "It's about time we had a drink."

While he was gone, Sally came out with something she had had on her mind all morning.

"Ian," she said tentatively, shyly, "would you mind very much if I didn't come to the airport with you? It's going to be so awful"—she stopped and swallowed—"I mean, I think I'd rather be here when you really go."

"Whatever you wish, Sally." Ian did seem to mind, and he didn't look at her.

"You always have to go on saying good-bye after it's already happened. You have to stand around . . ." Sally said, trying to explain, looking up at her aunt for confirmation.

"You're absolutely right, Sally. Charles and Ian can just tootle off by themselves and we'll stay here."

"No," Sally said firmly, "you go with them, Aunt Violet. Please do. Then Charles won't be lonely driving back, and . . ." but she did not finish her sentence. What she really wanted was to be here with the house alone.

"All right, darling, whatever you say . . ." For the least I can do, thought Violet, is this one small thing I have no wish to do.

"I feel so queer," Ian said suddenly. "I don't know what's happening to me."

"Nothing a drink won't cure," Charles came clattering and clinking through the door. It was true that the drinks made a tremendous difference. The edges which had been so sharp blurred a little and conversation which kept edging up to a point, to a question and then stopping short, now flowed with something like ease. Ian, in a last spurt, threw himself into the telling of various stories and Violet laughed almost continuously so there was an unbroken murmur around them. Sally felt she was floating a little above and beyond everything, a strangely peaceful place in which Charles, Ian and Violet seemed almost equally beautiful and she herself did not have to exist except to appreciate and glory in their beauty, not for herself, but for itself.

There was not a breath of wind so the trees looked, for once, perfectly still and at peace. The sheep had found shade and lay, close together, somnolent in the oak grove, giving an occasional querulous baa, then chewing their cuds as if the question had been answered.

"All my questions are answered except one," Sally said, getting up for the first time and standing very tall and straight. She was not looking at Violet or Charles or Ian. She was looking up at the house, at the tall open windows, at the formidable stone height over her head. She was asking her question of the house, so they all felt. "What is wrong with our lives?" she asked the house, half-smiling, and then quickly and piercingly glanced down at her aunt.

Violet was startled into an answer before she knew it. "Only very simple things," she said quietly, "like youth and age, innocence and sophistication, poverty and riches—"

"What are you talking about, Violet?" Charles said crossly. "The only thing that's wrong with my life is that I'm getting old," he said savagely.

"That's what I said," Violet murmured, "youth, age—"

"It isn't an answer," Sally said disdainfully. "It's an evasion."

But Ian was interested. "You mean," he asked Violet, "you learn the things too late. When you've had your life you know about it, is that it?"

"The house," Sally said, still standing absorbed in her contemplation, "means something else. It accuses us. I felt it the first time I ever came here—when I fell up the stairs. I wonder," she added half to herself, "if I'll ever make my peace with the house."

"You know, Violet," Charles said leaning forward, "this morning for the first time almost since we got here, I woke up and it felt like home. Now why is that?" he asked, turning the glass in his hand.

"Because you're making it," Sally said quickly, "you're inside. When I'm really inside something, I'll begin— I'll be—" she stammered. "Oh, how I hate college where no one is ever inside anything real!"

Maire opened the glass door and stuck her head out, "It's on the table," she said, blushing, "lunch," she said as if they might imagine it was tea or dinner.

"By Jove, yes," Charles looked at his watch. "It's time we fed, Violet, if we're not to have to hurry."

"But just stay a moment, just a second," Sally cried

out, as if it really mattered. And, startled into obedience, Charles sat down again. "I just want to look at you a second, forever," she said gravely. She looked at them one by one, Charles smiling at her, indulgent, puzzled, Ian quite still as if his picture were being taken, and Violet staring off at the sheep as if she had not heard and were just waiting passively for the moment to rise and go in. "There," Sally said, "you can move now."

In that instant they seemed to her unutterably dear and beautiful, but also about to vanish. They seemed like ghosts of themselves, attended by other ghosts, her father riding up, her great-grandmother and all the others, the great procession of Denes. They are all shadows, the house is substance, she thought, but now she was being pulled along by Charles, who was laughing, telling her she looked as if she had seen a ghost.

At the last moment Sally almost decided to go with them, as Ian's dark leather bag was lifted into the back, as he ran up the stairs to put a pound in Maire's hand, as he then turned, hesitated, might perhaps have kissed her but she luckily put out her hand and shook his quickly and could not say a word. Charles and Violet were already in the car.

"Well," he said. He said, "Sally—"

"Just go," Sally heard herself saying. "Don't try to say anything," and then as he turned away, she added, "Have a good flight!"

Before she knew what had happened the little black car had disappeared and she was left with one arm up, still waving but waving now at the trees, at the sheep, waving into space, alone like a mad person. She let her hand fall and stood there and then turned to go in, giving one searching glance at the wall of windows, at the stone height above her, a measuring glance which asked, "Can I do it?" almost as if she were about to scale them, and not as she did do, merely go into the house alone.

She went into the great hall and looked up at the portrait of her great-grandmother, and rested her eyes on the small elegant neck, on the bright dark eyes in the very oval face, on the surprising stubborn lower lip.

"You knew what you wanted," she said to herself. Yes, she had known what she wanted and yet she had not died here in the house after all.

It was now that the absolute silence rushed out around her so that for just a second she felt dizzy, as if she were dissolving and had herself become a ghost. Identity flowed away into that silence. It was a matter, she knew, instinctively now, of attack. She must not let herself be invaded by this silence. She must dominate it.

So she walked, she did not run to the backstairs and said to Annie quite quietly, "Annie, dear, do you suppose I could find an old pair of gloves somewhere? I need them."

"Whatever for, doatie? I'll take a look round, but first you'd better sit down and have a sip of tea." Annie was already on her way to the stove with a cup in her hand. But she was stopped by a kind of authority in Sally's voice.

"I really must have them now, Annie. You see, what I must do is to clear out those nettles in the stables. It's been on my mind for weeks."

Annie started to say something, gave one look at the set face in which determination had driven out all other feelings, and changed her mind. She disappeared into one of the many cupboards and came back holding out a pair of very dirty crumpled old brown cotton gloves.

"Would these be what you were looking for?" she asked with a barely perceptible twinkle in her eye.

"That's wonderful, thanks," Sally said and fled up the stairs again and out, running as if she would be fatally late for an appointment.

Well there are ways and ways of curing a broken heart, Annie was thinking, but pulling nettles is a new one. And she thought with satisfaction, she's a Dene all right. Characters every one of them. You never know what to expect.

But of course she was wrong. For Sally among the

nettles was happy, was for the moment fulfilled by something more than love. She was "inside" all that she had been outside of for so long, and she was inside it alone and free. Pulling out the nettles was the first gesture of a prisoner released.